The Wrong Miss Thompson

a Regency romance

by Philippa Carey

A similar, but shorter, version of this story was published in May 2020 by D. C. Thomson as People's Friend Pocket Novel #914, "A Suitable Companion".

This edition by Idyllic Books UK.

All enquiries to enquiries@idyllic-books.uk

Prologue

The butler opened the study door and stood aside for Claire to enter.

"Miss Thompson, sir," he announced.

"Take a seat, Miss Thompson," said the earl, waving to the chair in front of his desk. He didn't look at her, but continued reading a sheet of paper.

As she went to sit down, Claire could see his lordship was much younger than she had expected. Much better looking too. Very much better looking. She was going to be companion to Lady Sutton, and knew milady was an older lady. Claire had supposed milady's husband would be similarly old too. With his head bent down to read the document, she could see this man had a full head of wavy brown hair. It was not silver or getting thin on top which would not have been unusual in the older man whom she had anticipated. This one was surely less than thirty years old. He then, was unlikely to be Lady Sutton's husband. Was Lady Sutton a widow and this was her son? Nobody had mentioned she was a widow and why did he, not milady, want to see her this morning anyway?

Claire sat quietly with her hands in her lap, studying him while she waited for him to finish reading and give her his attention. Finally, he looked up and then blinked in surprise, seemingly astonished she was there. He sat back in his chair with eyebrows drawn together and stared at her.

1

"Miss Thompson?" he said at last, looking, and sounding, very puzzled. Almost as if she was not whom he had been expecting.

Chapter 1

It was a necessary evil. Claire Thompson recognised stagecoach travel was the only way to get to her employer, but she would never recommend it. It was slow, uncomfortable and grubby. The coach interior was smelly and she wondered if it was ever cleaned. Some of her fellow passengers were smelly too, but at least there was a chance of them getting out at one of the many stops. She wondered if the outside passengers appreciated the fresh air of which they had plenty. Not that she wanted to be amongst their number. It wasn't done for a young lady to ride on the roof and in any case, she would be in constant fear of falling off. Besides, there was a fine drizzle today and the outside passengers must be soaked by now. It was damp and a bit steamy inside too, but at least they weren't wet through.

How she wished she could afford to travel post or in a comfortable private carriage, or even by mail coach. But if she could afford to travel like that, she wouldn't need to travel to an employer in the first place, would she? No, her younger sister and two younger brothers meant she had to take employment to ease the strain on her family's declining fortunes. As it was, her brothers were going to a local school, not a famous one like Eton or Harrow.

The coach rumbled on, occasionally jolting as the wheels bumped across ruts in the road. The novelty of travelling by stagecoach had worn off yesterday and now she regretted not bringing a second book to read. The light was fading anyway and besides, reading was difficult with the erratic movement of the vehicle. It was all very tiring and very tedious. The view from the window seemed to be endless wet fields, wet trees and wet sheep. The view inside was equally uninspiring. She had three nondescript fellow passengers, who were not inclined to talk. Even when the passengers changed, it only made the atmosphere even more humid and oppressive, as a new passenger always seemed wetter than the departing passenger.

Claire longed for the journey to end, despite not knowing exactly what to expect at her destination. She supposed they would soon arrive at Stony Stratford, where she would at last leave the coach before being collected by one of her employer's servants. She glanced out of the window at the damp gloomy weather. If there wasn't someone already waiting for her, should she stand around in the drizzle of a wet inn yard? Or go into the inn which would be dry, but probably be full of people? If she went into the inn, she might be hard to find. After all, she wouldn't recognise her employer's servant and he wouldn't recognise her. Perhaps she should wait outside even if she got wet. In the letter, it said the house was only a few miles from Stony Stratford, but a companion most likely only merited a gig, so she was going to get wet anyway.

Finally, the noise of their travel changed as they entered the small town and the rattle of the wheels over the cobbles was reflected from the houses.

Moments later the coach slowed and turned into the yard of the Bull Inn where it stopped. It was suddenly noisy as the guard let down the steps and, as he opened the door, announced they had arrived at Stony Stratford. Claire left the coach and looked around the wet yard, as the ostlers busied themselves changing the horses. Her fellow passengers hurried into the inn where there was surely a warm fire and a hot drink.

"Miss Thompson?" said a voice behind her.

"Yes," she said, turning to face a young groom in a dripping hat and coat.

"If you would show me your bag miss, the carriage is outside in the street."

Claire pointed out her large portmanteau which had been taken from the boot and dropped onto the cobbles. The groom picked it up and hurried out of the yard, his shoulders hunched against the drizzle, followed by Claire. She was really grateful she wouldn't have to stand around for long in the rain. As they emerged into the street, she was surprised, and not a little relieved, to see the groom putting her bag into a smart gentleman's carriage. She wouldn't have a wet journey in the rain after all.

Claire settled back into the seat with a sigh. This was such an improvement. If the household sent a carriage like this to collect her ladyship's companion, then it suggested the house might be equally elegant and comfortable. If her ladyship had a pleasant personality too, Claire would be well content with her new position in life. Of course, there was no guarantee her employer would not be a bad tempered and disagreeable old lady, but at least this was an encouraging start. She felt the seat with her gloved hand and looked around the inside of the carriage. She was no expert, but it looked to her as if the vehicle was not only new but expensively made. The wood was glossy, the seat unmarked and the fittings highly polished brass. If Lady Sutton had a vehicle like this, it suggested she was not only wealthy but in the habit of travelling around. The prospect was so much better than Claire had hoped.

After a while, Claire started to wonder when they would reach their destination. In her engagement letter it had said the house was no more than a few miles from Stony Stratford. How many was 'a few' in this county? She had no way to tell the time, but if she had been told they had been travelling for more than an hour, she would not have disputed it. The light was almost completely gone now and if they didn't arrive soon, they would be travelling in the dark. With the light failing, the cloudy sky and continuing drizzle, it will soon be difficult to see their way. At least the road was smooth, or the coach was well sprung, she couldn't be sure. She supposed the coachman was familiar with the road and was unlikely to pitch them into the ditch.

Her nervous thoughts changed as the carriage suddenly slowed and turned between large and ornate gates. This must be the house, not that she could see anything much in the gloom. Claire soon realised she hadn't been able to see the house from the gateway, simply because the drive was very long.

As the carriage finally drew up in front of some wide horseshoe steps, she looked up and saw this was a very large house. The entrance portico was supported by half a dozen tall columns and the front of the house stretched off into the gloom to either side. Her eyes widened. Nothing had prepared her for a house of this size and magnificence. Lady Sutton must be very comfortably situated. Footmen hurried to let down the step and open the carriage door.

Claire hurried through the murky air up the steps to where a smartly dressed butler was holding open the door. Light streamed out from a brightly lit hall.

"Good evening, Miss Thompson?" he asked, as she stepped inside.

"Yes, I am Miss Thompson," she said, as she removed her bonnet.

"Very good, I am Mr Blake. Mrs Newsome the housekeeper will be here in a moment to show you to your room. We have guests this evening, so his lordship instructed me to tell you he will speak with you in the morning."

"Thank you, Mr Blake," said Claire, wondering for a moment why his lordship was going to be speaking with her in the morning. Presumably he was her employer's husband, but why him and not his wife? Was her ladyship infirm? Claire was sure her engagement letter had come from her ladyship, not her husband.

A plump lady in black bombazine with keys at her waist, clearly the housekeeper, arrived from the back of the house followed by a maid.

"Good evening Miss Thompson, I am Mrs Newsome, the housekeeper. I shall show you to your room in a moment. Have you eaten this evening?"

"No, I'm afraid not," replied Claire, shaking her head.

"No matter. Jean," she said to the maid, "ask cook for a tray for Miss Thompson and bring it upstairs when it is ready." She turned back to Claire, "follow me please Miss Thompson."

Mrs Newsome headed up the stairs, followed by Claire, who was in turn followed by a footman carrying her bag. They went up a floor and Claire could hear voices from one of the rooms, then they went up another floor to where she supposed the family had bedrooms. Then they went up yet another floor, where the carpets were not quite so fine. They made their way down a corridor and the housekeeper paused briefly at one door.

"This is the nursery," she said, moving on and pausing again at the next door, "and this is the schoolroom."

Claire wondered why she was being told this. Was it because they had so many guests, the rooms on the floor below were all occupied? Or was she being put on the nursery floor because she was the companion, not a family member and not entirely a servant either?

"And this is your room," said Mrs Newsome, opening the door and standing to one side.

Claire went in and looked around. It was certainly spacious and well furnished. The curtains were a bit faded and had probably been elsewhere originally. Some of the furniture was in an old style and had no doubt moved up from a lower floor at some time as well. However, it all looked clean and nothing was actually worn out. It might be on the nursery floor, but it appeared inviting and at least now she didn't have to share her room with her sister.

"It looks very comfortable."

The housekeeper smiled and nodded. "Good. Jean will be up shortly with a tray and I'll send someone up with a jug of hot water too. I expect you will be tired after your journey, so I'll say good night. In the morning, if you simply wander back downstairs, you will no doubt come across a maid or footman and they can show you to the breakfast room."

The footman stepped past them to deposit her bag on the floor.

"Thank you, Mrs Newsome, good night."

Mrs Newsome smiled and went out, just before Jean arrived with a tray which she put on a side table. The maid smiled at Claire and left, closing the door behind her.

Well, thought Claire, so far, so good. She tossed her pelisse, hat and gloves onto the bed before sitting down at the table. She hadn't managed to snatch more than a small bite to eat at the stagecoach stop in St Albans, so she was ready to do full justice to the food on the tray. It all looked very inviting too, so she sat down and eagerly made a start.

Philippa Carey

Chapter 2

In the morning, Claire found her way down to the breakfast room which, except for servants, was deserted when she arrived. She had had an early night and consequently woke up early too. She supposed the guests, by contrast, had had a late night and consequently would not appear until later.

She inspected the chafing dishes on the sideboard and a footman added items to a plate for her. Her tray last night had been very tasty and now she looked forward to her breakfast. At home the food was sufficient, but little more, so Claire was in the habit of eating all she was given, not simply pecking at it. As she sat, the butler poured a cup of coffee for her.

"Good morning Miss Thompson," he said, "his lordship asks you to attend him in his study when you have finished your breakfast. As soon as you are ready, I will show you the way."

She nodded. "Thank you Mr Blake."

As she ate, Claire wondered again why the early rising Lord Sutton wanted to see her. She had supposed Lady Sutton would arise late and then she would be taken to meet her. So why did Lord Sutton want to see her instead? Well, she would find out soon enough.

Finally, after a very satisfying breakfast and two cups of exceedingly good coffee, she rose from the table. If nothing else, she thought she was going to enjoy mealtimes in this house. She would have to restrain her appetite if she was not to get fat.

Mr Blake came forward from where he had been standing in the corner of the room. She followed him down a hallway and around a corner where he stopped in front of a door. Tapping on the panel, he opened the door and stood aside for Clair to enter.

"Miss Thompson, sir," he announced.

"Take a seat, Miss Thompson," said the earl, waving to the chair in front of his desk. He continued reading a sheet of paper.

As she went to sit down, Claire could see his lordship was much younger than she had expected. Much better looking too. Very much better looking. She was going to be companion to Lady Sutton, and knew milady was an older lady. Claire had supposed milady's husband would be similarly old too. With his head bent down to read the document, she could see this man had a full head of wavy brown hair. It was not silver or getting thin on top which would not have been unusual in the older man whom she had anticipated. This man was surely less than thirty years old. He then, was unlikely to be Lady Sutton's husband. Was Lady Sutton a widow and this was her son? Nobody had mentioned she was a widow and she still wondered why did he, not milady, want to see her this morning anyway?

Claire sat quietly with her hands in her lap, studying him while she waited for him to finish reading and give her his attention. Finally, he looked up and then blinked in surprise, seemingly astonished she was there. He sat back in his chair with eyebrows drawn together and stared at her.

"Miss Thompson?" he said at last, looking, and sounding, very puzzled. Almost as if she was not whom he had been expecting.

David, The Earl Barton, was glad to hear the new governess had arrived last night as expected. Hopefully she would be more successful than the last one, who had given notice two weeks ago and then left rather suddenly. He knew his young daughter, Lady Mary, was difficult, which probably stemmed from the lack of a loving mother. She had a nursemaid, but now she was growing up, a governess as well was essential. And having a house full of guests, such as just at the moment, was a very inconvenient time to be without a governess. A daughter liable to tantrums was not going to endear him, or her, to Miss Hawksley, one of their guests. Keeping prospective stepmother and stepdaughter apart would not make sense, so he really hoped the new governess could calm the waters.

This time he had hired an older lady with long experience as a governess. Miss Thompson came strongly recommended by the agency and was only looking for a new post as her previous charges were now old enough to make their come-out. Her previous employer, a marchioness, had apparently written a very flattering reference.

He had said to Blake to bring her to see him, after she had breakfasted, so he could explain to her about Mary, her capricious nature and the need for discretion in front of his visitors. Then he would take her up to the nursery and introduce them to each other before joining his guests at breakfast. In the meantime, he had some peace and quiet to deal with this morning's letters.

There was a gentle tap on the door, which then opened quietly.

"Miss Thompson, sir," announced Blake.

"Take a seat, Miss Thompson," said David, waving to the chair in front of his desk, as he finished reading a letter. The letter finished, he put it to one side, so as to reply later. He looked up. There was a very pretty young lady sitting there, regarding him quietly.

Who on earth was this? Blake had announced her as Miss Thompson. Miss Thompson, the governess whom he was expecting, was forty-something years old with decades of experience. This lady appeared to be about twenty years old and could not possibly have the expected decades of experience. She was quite decidedly pretty, with curly black hair held back from her face by a blue ribbon. She had a slender neck and her dress was a royal blue with a little lace around her collar. Her dress was smart, without being extravagant. She was sitting very straight in the chair, but did not look like a governess. Definitely not. By no stretch of the imagination would any casual observer suppose she was a governess. Governesses were supposed to be older, plain featured spinsters with plain grey dresses and plain hair pulled back into a severe bun. David frowned in confusion. Had he misheard his butler? He hadn't really been paying close attention. If this wasn't Miss Thompson, which seemed unlikely, who on earth was she?

"Miss Thompson?"

"Yes, milord," she replied with a small smile, "I am Miss Thompson, her ladyship's new companion."

Companion? His mother had engaged a companion? No, no, something wasn't right. She had definitely said she was Miss Thompson. He was expecting Miss Thompson to be a governess for his daughter, not a companion for his mother. He was also expecting Miss Thomson to be twice the age of this lady and nothing like as pretty. He rang the bell on his desk and a footman appeared in the doorway.

"Please ask the countess to come and see me as soon as possible."

"Yes, sir," said the footman who hurried away.

David studied Miss Thompson for a few moments more before opening a desk drawer and removing a letter. He was not dreaming. According to this letter, Miss Thompson was a lady of forty seven years of age with over twenty years of service as a governess. He looked up again at Claire. She was regarding him steadily and quietly from disconcertingly dark brown eyes. This was obviously not the Miss Thompson he was expecting, although she was claiming to have that name. Furthermore, she definitely said she was his mother's new companion, not a governess. Something here wasn't making any sense.

The door opened and his mother, the dowager

countess, came in. She only took a couple of steps before seeing Claire and then turning an enquiring gaze on her son.

"What is it Barton? Why do you need me in such a hurry?"

David had risen to his feet, as had Claire. Claire dropped a curtsey.

"Mother, have you neglected to tell me you have engaged a companion?" He indicated Claire.

"A companion? No, I have no need of a companion and if I did, I would have told you."

Claire looked from one to the other, now looking as puzzled as his lordship.

"Miss Thompson, if that is your name, you say you have been engaged as companion to her ladyship?" asked his lordship.

"Yes, sir. I have a letter in my room offering me the post of companion to Lady Elizabeth Sutton," she said, indicating the dowager, although somewhat hesitantly.

"Ah," said David, "I see there has been some confusion somewhere. Exactly how, where or why, I do not know, but no doubt it will become clear very soon. This is not Lady Sutton, this is my mother, the Dowager Countess Barton. I'm afraid I'm not acquainted with a Lady Sutton."

Claire stared at him in astonishment and her mouth dropped open. She looked at her ladyship. This wasn't Lady Sutton? She was Dowager Countess Barton? She had called him 'Barton', so almost certainly he must be Earl Barton. She looked at his lordship again. Where on earth was she? She must be in the wrong house, but how could this have happened? She closed her mouth and, for a moment, her eyes too. It was like a bad dream. No, not a dream, it was a nightmare. She took a deep breath to recover her composure.

"So," she said, recovering her wits and standing up straight, "if you are not Lady Sutton, then doubtless this is not Sutton Hall in the village of Wicken. In which case, where am I?"

"No," said the dowager, "I'm afraid we are not in Wicken. This is Hemingford Park in the village of Emberton. Wicken is some thirty miles west of here, towards Buckingham." She gestured vaguely in a direction which must have been approximately west.

Claire's shoulders slumped. This was not just a nightmare, it was a complete disaster. She sat down heavily in the chair, even though her ladyship remained standing. She was in the wrong house, in the wrong village, with the wrong people. How could this have happened? Just when she thought she had fallen on her feet and found a comfortable post. What would Lady Sutton say when Claire arrived late? How much of a stickler for punctuality might she be? Would she be angry? Would Claire be turned away and have to go all the way back to Kent on the stagecoach? How was she going to get to Wicken anyway?

"Barton, ring the bell and call for coffee," said the dowager, "I think we all need to sit around the table and work out what has happened." Lady Barton approached Claire. "Come my dear, this is confusing for both of us too. Do not be so distressed, I'm sure we can get to the bottom of it."

The three of them went to the chairs at the end of the room, which were arranged around a coffee table. Large bay windows with diamond panes of glass gave a view onto the soaking wet gardens, although nobody was very interested in the view just at the moment. The coffee arrived very promptly. It had, after all, only been a short distance away in the breakfast room.

"Miss Thompson, tell me about your arrival at Stony Stratford," said the earl, once they were seated and had a cup of coffee in front of each of them.

"Well, sir," said Claire, "I arrived on the stagecoach from London. No sooner had I descended into the yard of the inn than your man asked me if I was Miss Thompson. I said I was, he took my bag and led me to your coach which was standing outside in the street. We came here. It was dark, so I had no idea where we were going, besides I don't know the countryside in this area."

"Did he ask if you were the Miss Thompson going to Hemingford Park?"

"No sir, he just asked if I was Miss Thompson. He was in bit of a hurry. It was not surprising really, as it was raining and starting to get dark. No doubt he was keen to arrive before the night was pitch black and he wouldn't be able to see the road."

She didn't want to get the coachman into trouble, since he had been perfectly pleasant, helpful and besides, had saved her from standing around in the rain.

The earl nodded his understanding.

"There are a huge number of stagecoaches which stop at Stony Stratford, so a degree of confusion is to be expected in the normal run of things," he said, "In the circumstances, the coachman deserves a reprimand for not taking more care, but I take your point about the rain, the dark and his consequent hurry. In addition, I suppose he was not to expect there would be two Miss Thompsons arriving at about the same time, which was a very unfortunate coincidence."

"Two Miss Thompsons?" asked the countess.

"Well, obviously!" said David. "Lady Sutton must now be wondering why Miss Thompson is a governess of mature years instead of the young companion she was expecting."

The countess looked at Claire thoughtfully. An experienced and older governess would definitely be preferable just at the moment, so as to keep her fractious and volatile granddaughter out of everyone's way. Somebody who knew how to deal well with small children. Not only this, but if her son was paying court to Miss Hawksley, it would be unhelpful to have this pretty young lady around the house. It could cause all sorts of complications. Who knew what Miss Hawksley might think? It would be enormously embarrassing if she supposed this Miss Thompson was David's mistress. It was out of the question David would have a mistress in his own house, but so far Miss Hawksley didn't seem very bright and apparently she entertained some rather odd ideas. She had been told yesterday a new and older governess was expected at any moment and her mother, Lady Hawksley, appeared to think her daughter's approval was required. It was none of her daughter's business until she became Lady Barton and the countess didn't think this was by any means a foregone conclusion, even if Miss Hawksley and her mother thought it was so. Regardless, the sooner this wrong Miss Thompson was bundled off to Wicken, in exchange for the other one, the better.

"I think, Barton, you must have your carriage sent around as soon as possible, so this Miss Thompson may be conveyed to Wicken and exchanged for the other Miss Thompson."

"Milady," said Claire, "I can see there might be a possibility Lady Sutton could object to me arriving late and might also take a dim view of me willingly getting into a stranger's carriage in the evening."

She turned to the earl, "I mean no offence my lord, but I don't know how she might view it. If she took a high moral standpoint, she might turn me away. If she does, I must ask for your carriage to return me to Stony Stratford on it's way back here. I must also beg a loan of the return fare back to my home in Kent. My father will not hesitate to refund the loan."

Lady Barton could see her point. She didn't know this Lady Sutton and, for all she knew, the lady might really be a high stickler, especially if she was getting on in years. If she was engaging a companion, there was a good chance she actually was aged and possibly old fashioned too. Since the mistake was by Barton's servant, this Miss Thompson should not be penalised as a result.

"Of course," said the countess, "this will not be a problem, but you will not need a loan, we will pay your fare. Who is your father?"

"He is Baron Hunton, milady."

"Indeed?" said the countess. So this young lady is the daughter of a peer, she thought, but obviously a peer in financial difficulties, if he allows a daughter of her age to leave home and become a companion. Despite this, her dress was well cut, although it was simple and most likely made by a provincial seamstress. As well, it seemed her family did not have a maid they could spare as a chaperone for the journey. Presumably this Lady Sutton must be of rank too, to take a baron's daughter as companion. Why did she not know her? Lady Barton resolved to look her up in Debrett's Peerage. She would also look up Baron Hunton too, whilst she had the book in her hands. In the meantime, all the more reason to remove a lady who is both attractive and possibly eligible, but bit of an unknown, from sight around the house. Miss Hawksley was a known quantity and her family was a very desirable political connection too, even if she might have feathers in her head.

"Just a moment, mother," said David, "we could certainly send this Miss Thompson off in the carriage, but I think we are duty bound to send an explanation too. After all, this fiasco is our servant's mistake, not anybody else's. I think either you or I should go with her to apologise to Lady Sutton."

"Unnecessary and impossible too. We have guests who arrived only yesterday. Neither of us can simply abandon them for the day while a foolish mistake is corrected. What would they think?"

"This is very true, and in any case, other things occur to me. We are assuming Lady Sutton has also discovered by now what has occurred. However, we are, as well, assuming the other Miss Thompson hasn't gone completely astray. Finally, we don't know if Lady Sutton will cut up stiff about it, as this Miss Thompson has just mentioned as a possibility. If our carriage was to go haring off to Wicken with this Miss Thomson, while the other Miss Thompson was coming the other way in Lady Sutton's carriage, the whole affair could descend into farce."

Silence descended while they all mulled it over and drank their coffee.

The dowager could see his point. It was bad enough having an incompetent servant, but she wouldn't want tales of a farce getting around at their expense. Not only this, but it looked as if they were wronging a gently bred young lady, through no fault of her own, and this was intolerable too.

"Miss Thompson," said the dowager, "I wonder if we could prevail on you to stay for today and perhaps tomorrow too? We shall write to this Lady Sutton, explain the mishap and suggest the two of you be exchanged at Stony Stratford at a mutually agreed time and date. In the interim, perhaps you would undertake to be a companion to my granddaughter Lady Mary? As you have probably gathered, we have important guests in the house for the next few days. My granddaughter is only five years old and at present a difficult child, prone to tempers and tantrums. We don't wish her to upset or disturb our guests, so it is more a question of keeping her amused and out of the way, rather than trying to educate her or instill good manners. Do you have any experience of dealing with small children?"

"Oh yes, milady, I have a younger sister and two younger brothers."

"Excellent. Well then, is this an agreeable proposal while we sort everything out? Naturally we will recompense you for assisting us in this way."

Claire didn't need to give it much thought. She had nothing else to do, did she? For a day or two she would live in comfort with people who seemed amenable and who also had a good cook. She would be paid and, all being well, perhaps generously too. All she had to do was play games with a small girl in the nursery. It sounded easy. Possibly too easy. It seemed as if the girl might be spoilt and bad tempered, but Claire could surely put up with her for a very short while, couldn't she? At the end of the day, apparently she just had to keep herself and the girl out of sight of the guests. Then Claire wondered why? Her ladyship had effectively said the child's behaviour was embarrassing, but surely the girl wasn't deformed or deranged in some way? Well, whatever the reason, it was only for a day or so in any case.

"Yes, milady, I shall be glad to help while I am here. As I understand it, I am to keep Lady Mary entertained and out of everybody's way in the nursery floor, is that correct? And where should I take my meals?"

"I think it would be simplest if you were to join

Mary at mealtimes in the nursery. It would save us complicated explanations to our guests."

"Very good, milady. Shall I go and meet Lady Mary now?"

If the child was deranged, or violent, or something equally terrible, it was best if she found out straightaway, so she could then change her mind if necessary.

"Allow me to take you upstairs and introduce you," said David, rising to his feet and heading for the door.

As they reached the nursery floor, he turned to Claire. "I should perhaps explain that her mother, my wife, died from a fever some three years ago. Mary found it difficult to understand and she has been over-indulged and excessively pampered by everyone ever since. Now her behaviour has become somewhat ingrained. Her governess tried to correct it, but without success, and finally abandoned the attempt two weeks ago and left rather suddenly."

As they reached the nursery door, they heard a small girl's voice shrieking, "I don't want to and I shan't! Take it away, I don't like it."

The earl took a deep breath and opened the door.

Chapter 3

"Good morning Mary, I have brought someone to meet you," he said.

"Papa, nurse says I must wear my pink dress and I don't want to," said a small girl. She was a pretty child with curly blonde hair, but with crossed arms, a pout and a mutinous expression.

"Why don't you want to wear it?" said the earl, caught off-guard.

"Because I don't like it," was the strident reply.

He sighed. "Which one do you want to wear?"

"The blue one."

"Very well, you may wear the blue." He nodded to Maisie the nursemaid, who took the pink dress back to the clothes press.

"While nurse is getting your blue dress, I would like you to meet someone. This is Miss Thompson. Miss Thompson, this is my daughter Lady Mary."

Lady Mary looked at Claire with a scowl. "I don't want another governess. Governesses are horrid and cruel."

"Oh, but I'm not a governess," said Claire, with her hand on her chest for emphasis. She was relieved to find the girl wasn't deformed or deranged, as she had feared. It appeared Lady Mary was simply spoilt, at a difficult age and had probably had her own way for far too long. If she could deal with a demanding younger sister, she was sure she could manage this girl too, even if she was a more extreme case.

"I'm just a visitor here for a day or two. I don't have anything to do, so your papa said I might come and talk to you."

The nurse dropped a blue dress over Mary's head. Claire took the opportunity to turn to the earl and make shooing motions with her hands. He opened his mouth to speak, but Claire shook her head and shooed him towards the door. He closed his mouth and raised an eyebrow, but backed out of the room, closing the door quietly behind himself.

As Mary's head emerged from the dress, she went to speak, but then looked around. "Papa? Where is my papa?"

"He went to see to his guests," said Claire, "I'm sure he thought we could manage perfectly well on our own."

Mary stamped a foot and crossed her arms again, while the nurse did up the buttons at the back of Mary's dress. "He has to come back and take you away. I don't want another governess."

"But I'm not a governess, I've never been a governess and I don't want to be a governess either," said Claire, "and I'm only going to be here until tomorrow, so I can't possibly be your governess, can I?"

Mary viewed Claire with narrowed eyes and a frown.

"Why are you only here until tomorrow? Aren't you one of papa's guests?"

"No, I was brought here by mistake, there was a mix-up and I'm supposed to be in a house somewhere else. I shall be going there tomorrow."

In view of what she had learned so far, Claire thought it might be unwise to explain she was going to be exchanged tomorrow for a governess. When this little girl found out this was the case, there would undoubtedly be tears and tantrums. Claire expected to be far away when this happened. However, she couldn't help wondering why Lady Mary was so dead set against having another governess.

"Why," said Claire, "don't you want a governess?"

"Because they're nasty and smack my fingers with a ruler when I get my letters wrong."

Ah! Thought Claire. So the last one was probably impatient and unkind. It was unfortunate too, because at Mary's age, she no doubt needed to learn many things and her nursemaid was unlikely to be capable of teaching her. It was a difficult situation, but not one where Claire could be of much help, since she wouldn't be here for more than a day or so.

"Oh well. That's not nice, not nice at all. I certainly wouldn't smack your fingers, even if I was your governess, which I'm not of course. If you don't want to practice your letters, I'm not going to make you. No, I thought we could play a game or I could read you a story. I only brought one book with me to read in the stagecoach and I finished it before we were halfway here. I was hoping you might have something I could read to you."

"You came in a stagecoach?"

"Yes, from my home in Kent to London and then in another stagecoach from London to Stony Stratford."

"Why didn't you come in your own carriage?"

"My papa doesn't have a carriage. He only has one horse and a gig for going into town."

"Only one horse?" exclaimed Mary with a

grimace, as if it was a very odd idea. "My papa has a huge stable with lots and lots of horses. Why doesn't your papa have more than one horse?" She frowned again for a moment, before her face cleared into a smile. "I have my very own pony."

Claire's lack of transport was obviously of little interest.

"You have a pony? How lovely, what's her name?"

"She's called Moonbeam because she's all white. I'm learning to ride her."

Claire was relieved the subject of governesses had been forgotten, at least for the moment. Horses sounded like a safer topic. "She sounds beautiful, does your papa teach you?"

"Papa? No, he is always too busy. Fingle the head groom is the one who teaches me because he is the best groom."

"Do you suppose you could take me to see her later on?" Claire hoped they could do this without being spotted by the earl's guests.

"Let's go now!"

"No, not now, it's still chilly and damp outside. Let's go later when it's a bit warmer." This would also give Claire time to make sure they wouldn't be seen going to or in the stables. It seemed faintly ridiculous to be hiding from other people, but her instructions were clear enough.

"Does this mean I have to do my letters now?" said Mary, once more regarding Claire suspiciously through narrowed eyes.

Claire shook her head emphatically. She wasn't going to invite conflict. "Oh no, no, no. Well, only if you want to, but not if you don't. You could show me your toys or I could read you a story. What would you like to do?"

Mary looked surprised at the freedom she was being offered. "Would you like to see my dolls?"

"Yes, please," said Claire, "I haven't played with a doll for absolutely ages. I used to have a doll myself, but I gave it to my little sister. I don't think she plays with it any more now either. She's fifteen years old and she says she's much too old for dolls."

Claire was dragged by the hand across the room to a shelf upon which sat three very grand looking dolls with porcelain faces and frilly dresses.

"Goodness," said Claire, "what beautiful dolls. What are their names?"

"Jemima, Judith and Jane. Shall I get them down?"

Claire blinked. She hoped she wouldn't have to remember which one was which. She felt as if she was on thin ice as it was. "Why don't I sit on the sofa over there?" she said, pointing, "then you can get them down one at a time. We can sit together while you show each of them to me and tell me all about them?"

Philippa Carey

Chapter 4

David returned downstairs, back to his study, in a thoughtful frame of mind. His mother was still there, waiting for him.

"You are back soon," said the dowager, "was Mary still asleep?"

"By no means. She was objecting, quite forcefully, to the dress which the nursemaid had chosen for her."

"Oh dear. So did you thrust Miss Thompson into the room and beat a hasty retreat?"

"Not quite. Miss Thompson seemed to take in the situation at a glance and then she sent me packing. She did not appear to be at all alarmed at the scene, instead, she gave the impression of being able to take charge and deal with Mary with no assistance whatsoever from me."

"Perhaps her experience with younger brothers and a sister serves her well. Let us be grateful for small mercies and hope she endures until the other Miss Thompson gets here."

"Speaking of which, I must write at once to Lady Sutton to arrange an exchange. I'll send a groom and tell him to wait for a reply. If he goes now, he can be back here by this evening."

"Good," said the dowager rising and heading for the door. "I see the rain has stopped and the sky has cleared." She waved at the scene beyond the windows. "I suggest we visit the gardens of Castle Ashby as we had thought to do tomorrow, but go this afternoon, while the weather holds. Who knows what the weather will do in the next few days."

"An excellent idea. If you would suggest this to the Hawksley family, I will arrange for the carriages. Do you think it would be acceptable for me to take Miss Hawksley in my curricle whilst you follow in the landau with her parents?"

The dowager nodded her approval. "Yes, perfectly, provided you stay within sight of the our carriage, then there will be no question of impropriety and yet you will be able to speak privately with Miss Hawksley, although of course you will have a groom up behind you. The outing will also conveniently put distance between our visitors and the girls upstairs."

The groom sent with the letter, the carriages ordered and luncheon about to be served, David thought it prudent to go up to the nursery and observe the situation. He hesitated outside the door of the nursery and listened. There was a murmur of voices and it all sounded calm. He opened the door halfway and stuck his head inside. Mary, Miss Thompson and three dolls were all sitting around a table. On the table were plates, one of which held tiny sandwiches, and a number of small glasses.

"Papa!" cried Mary, with joy in her face, "look, we're having a luncheon party!"

David opened the door fully. Whatever he had expected to find, this wasn't it. He raised an eyebrow at Miss Thompson who appeared to be suppressing laughter as she looked at him. Possibly at the astonishment which was undoubtedly written on his face. He felt his spirits lift as he viewed the scene.

"Yes, indeed," he said, "I hope your dolls are behaving nicely and enjoying their luncheon too."

"Yes papa, and afterwards I'm going to take Miss Thompson to see Moonbeam."

"Very well, Mary, but only after your nap and if your father says you may," said Claire, with a meaningful look at his lordship.

"We are going for a carriage ride with our visitors this afternoon," he said to Mary, "so after your nap, it should be quiet in the stables and you may take Miss Thompson to see Moonbeam. If you wear your riding habit, Fingle will take you for a riding lesson. I shall send him a message to expect you."

He looked at Claire, who nodded her understanding.

"Everything well, Miss Thompson?"

"Yes, thank you my lord, we are getting along very nicely."

"Miss Thompson isn't a governess, papa," added Mary, "she told me so. I like her much better than a governess."

David looked at Miss Thompson who was blushing with embarrassment at Mary's forthright remark. David smiled, trying himself this time, not to laugh.

"Very good, I'm pleased, I will see you later," he said, closing the door and heading downstairs in a thoughtful frame of mind. He was feeling relieved at the way the arrangement seemed to be working, at least so far. In fact, much better than he had expected. Both of the young ladies in front of him had looked as if they were enjoying themselves, which was a blessed relief from the fraught scenes of a week ago. He resolved to return after the carriage ride to see how they were getting on.

Chapter 5

David handed Miss Hawksley into his curricle whilst a groom held the horses. He went around to the other side, climbed in and took the reins before nodding to the groom to let them go. The groom leapt up behind them. David held the horses back while he waited for the others to be ready.

"This is a splendid vehicle my lord," said Miss Hawksley, "but I trust you will not drive too fast?" She put her hand on his sleeve and looked up at him with a worried look on her face.

He looked back down at her. She made an enchanting picture in a rose pink carriage dress. Her matching bonnet was tied under her chin with a large bow. David did wonder if the amount of lace and the number of flounces and furbelows on her dress was a trifle excessive. However, her mother was dressed in a similar way, so perhaps it was the fashion, and what did he know about it anyway? He supposed it didn't matter, as long as frills flapping in the breeze didn't frighten the horses. Her blonde hair fell in artful ringlets either side of her face. As he looked at her face again, he could she was clearly nervous, but why?

"Never fear, Miss Hawksley, your parents will be following us in the landau and we will be driving at the same pace as them. I assure you that I am, in any case, a careful driver and would not dream of putting you at risk."

She glanced behind them and saw the others getting into the landau. "Thank you my lord. Other gentlemen have driven me at such a great speed I have been quite terrified by the experience. I'm sure I can trust someone like you." She looked up at him with a little smile and fluttered her eyelids.

David hoped she wouldn't be simpering and flirting all the way there. He wasn't really in the mood for it. He was a little nervous himself, but not of the drive. Although everything seemed more than peaceful at the moment with Mary, he worried the house might be in uproar when they returned. It had happened before. Miss Thompson wasn't a governess, so could she really cope? It was one thing to deal with Mary when she was in a good mood, but what about when she wasn't? Still, there wasn't anything he could do about it until he got back, so he tried to put it from his mind and concentrate on the outing with Miss Hawksley.

He considered the journey. It was no more than an hour, the road was good and the weather fine after the drizzle of yesterday. On the basis of his acquaintance with Miss Hawksley so far, intelligent conversation might be too much to hope for. Perhaps trivial nonsense might be better anyway, at least then he wouldn't have to concentrate on it and he could focus on the driving. He looked behind them and saw the others were ready, so he started the curricle moving up the drive.

Miss Hawksley clutched at his arm.

He wondered at the way she seemed excessively timid. She couldn't possibly be frightened of being alone with him. After all, her parents were just behind them and there was a groom sitting on the back too. Then too, the horses were only walking at this time. He considered his passenger. He had only spoken briefly to her yesterday and he had supposed then she was a little shy. If not shy, then perhaps intimidated at being brought here as a prospective bride for himself, an earl with a large house and estate. However, it could be she was simply of a rather fainthearted disposition and this was why she was nervous about travelling in his curricle. Her mother appeared to be a forceful character, so perhaps this girl was afraid to express herself? It was time he found himself a new countess, but it was no good him developing affection for a girl unable to cope as the mistress of a big house in the country and another in London, never mind the inevitable social demands on Countess Barton. This drive might be a chance for her to speak freely without being overheard by her parents. Hopefully she could show some character if she was away from them. If they married, her mother would definitely not be living in the same house. Unfortunately he had already some grave doubts it was her mother overwhelming her. He was fast forming the impression instead that she was simply a ninny. Maybe he was wrong, but he needed to find out. If nothing else, this outing might be a chance to get a true measure of her, without an overbearing mother getting in the way.

"Tell me, Miss Hawksley, do you enjoy riding? I have a large stable and without doubt I can find a horse which would suit you."

"I enjoy riding if the company is agreeable, and if

you have a gentle mare, then I'm sure I would find a ride pleasant."

"I see. Nothing too spirited then?"

"On no, my lord, if the horse is too excitable I can't enjoy the ride, as I am in constant fear of falling off. I know it is silly, but from the top of a horse, the ground looks so far away."

David concentrated on making the turn out of their drive onto the road towards the town of Olney. They had only just left his grounds, but he was already feeling more than a bit disappointed with Miss Hawksley. By the sound of it, if they were to go for a ride tomorrow, they would have to borrow Mary's pony for Miss Hawksley to ride. It was ridiculous. Mary was already an enthusiastic, if inexperienced rider of her pony. Could she be an example or inspiration for Miss Hawksley? No, such an idea was absurd. He enjoyed riding and was sure he would enjoy it more in the company of his countess, especially if she was as attractive as Miss Hawksley. Or as attractive as Miss Thompson, a little voice said to him. He shook the thought from his head. Miss Thompson was a temporary servant and would be gone tomorrow.

Within the hour, they had arrived at Castle Ashby and started to saunter around the famous gardens. While they were doing so, a couple of footmen who had followed in a governess cart were setting out some chairs and an afternoon tea.

"Miss Hawksley, have you visited these gardens before?" asked David.

"No my lord, but Lady Barton said they were very fine, so I am grateful you have brought me to see them."

"Are your gardens at home large too?"

"Oh, yes, they are."

David waited for her to say more, but she didn't.

"As large as the gardens at Hemingford Park?" he asked.

"As large as at Hemingford Park? I couldn't say as I have not seen them yet," she replied.

David could see a conversation was going to be hard work. He sagged mentally. She had been quiet on the journey here, perhaps nervous about riding in a curricle. However, it seemed Miss Hawksley was not only frightened of horses and travelling fast, but she was not a scintillating conversationalist either. Not very observant either, if she hadn't seen the gardens by looking out of the window. Why did his mother invite the Hawksleys? Was Miss Hawksley recommended for her beauty by one of his mother's friends? He knew many marriages were convenient arrangements between titled families, but this girl would bore him to tears within a week. Fortunately they were not staying for a week and any return invitation to visit the Hawksley's would have to be politely declined. In the meantime, he just needed to remain courteous and enjoy the visit to Castle Ashby himself.

While Lady Mary had been napping, Claire had found a window looking out on to the front of the house. The long drive was lined with trees and behind them were fences. Beyond them were sheep scattered across large meadows. She supposed the formal gardens were at the back of the house, which she had glimpsed from the windows when they had taken coffee. She looked down to see carriages sitting on the drive which curved around a fountain at the front of the house. She could see a young lady being handed in to a curricle and an older couple, with the dowager, being helped into a landau. Now she understood why Lady Mary was being kept out of sight. It appeared a beautiful blonde lady might be the earl's betrothed or soon-to-be-betrothed. A lady who would probably have second thoughts about a betrothal if faced with a potential step-daughter making strident demands or having a tantrum in front of her.

As they drove away, Claire knew they could now go down to the stables, but there was no need to wake Lady Mary. Instead, Claire might have a short nap herself. Keeping the girl entertained this morning had not been especially difficult, but it was certainly tiring. She supposed she hadn't got tired like this with her siblings, as she had been able to simply tell them to go away. She no longer had that choice.

Claire was dreaming. She had fallen in love with a handsome prince but an old witch had appeared from nowhere to drag her away and make her work as a drudge in her house. A small girl was pulling at her arm, trying to stop her being taken away by the witch.

"Miss Thompson, Miss Thompson," said Mary, shaking Claire's arm. "It's time to go and see

Moonbeam."

Claire shook herself awake as she remembered where she was. She saw Mary was already wearing a miniature riding habit, complete with hat.

"Just a moment, Lady Mary," said Claire, "let me put my half boots on and find a shawl, then we shall go. You will have to show me the way to the stables because I don't know where they are."

Minutes later, they descended the main staircase, hand in hand. At the bottom they came across Mr Blake who gave them a smile and a small bow. Claire returned the smile before being hurriedly dragged down a hallway leading to an outside door, presumably the one nearest the stables.

As they got close to the stables, Mary let go of Claire's hand and ran inside.

"Fingle, where are you? I've come for my riding lesson," she called out.

"Here I am, Lady Mary," said a grizzled old groom, emerging from the shadows. He saw Claire coming and touched his hat in salute. "Good afternoon Miss Thompson," he said, before turning his attention back to Mary.

Claire supposed everybody knew who she was by now, so at least she wouldn't have to offer any complicated explanations. No doubt she had been a topic of conversation in the servants' hall.

"Now then, Lady Mary, you take this, then go and say hello to Moonbeam," said Fingle, handing a small wrinkled apple to Mary. She raced away further into the stable.

"Will you be riding as well, miss?" he asked

41

Claire.

"No, I'm afraid not. I have never been taught and have no riding habit either, but I shall be interested to see what goes on."

"Very good miss, does his lordship want you to learn as well?"

"No, unfortunately not. I wish I could, but no, I shall be here only another day or so." She sighed, "I really would love to learn, but it can't happen."

"Very good miss," he said, "let me show you to Lady Mary's pony. Mind where you tread, it should be clean but it's a bit slippery what with the washing water and the cobbles."

They followed Mary into the stable but at a more normal pace. They could see Mary hopping excitedly from one foot to another as a groom opened the stall, and brought the pony out. Mary couldn't wait and gave the apple to the pony before wrapping her arms around its neck and pressing her cheek against it.

"She loves Moonbeam doesn't she?" said Claire to Fingle.

"Aye, she does miss. It's a pleasure to teach her."

"Will you be going far with her?"

"No miss, I'll have 'em trot around the paddock t'day, so you can stand by the fence and watch."

"Thank you Fingle, I shall enjoy it, I'm sure."

A short while later Claire watched them circling the paddock, Fingle jogging at their side with a rope to the bridle in his hand. Moonbeam was indeed all white with a flowing mane and tail. Mary's curls were bouncing up and down as she rode. There was pure delight on her face. Claire thought Mary and her pony made an enchanting picture. Of course, thought Claire, it was easy to like Mary when the child was doing something she enjoyed and wanted to do. It remained to be seen what would happen when Mary was asked to do something which she did not want to do.

Such an event was not long in coming.

They eventually came to a halt at the gate from the paddock.

"There you are Lady Mary, you did very well, but that's all for today," said Fingle.

"No, I want to do some more," said Mary, frowning and crossing her arms.

"Mary," said Claire, "I thought you did marvellously, you ride Moonbeam beautifully."

Mary looked at her, looking pleased at the praise.

"Why don't we go upstairs now and ask cook to send up some milk and cakes? Then you and Moonbeam can both have a little rest and perhaps do some more tomorrow." She glanced at Fingle who gave her a small nod.

"Then, while you're having your rest I could read you a story."

Mary narrowed her eyes as she considered this alternative. Claire decided to try a little more encouragement before Mary could take it into her head to rebel.

"Then when your papa comes back, we can tell him how well you were riding today."

"Where is my papa?" asked Mary, looking around as if he might be hovering nearby.

"He went for a ride in the carriage with your

visitors," said Claire, not knowing much more than this. She sensed she might have won this little skirmish and held up her hands to hold Mary. Mary slid off the pony into Claire's arms and put her own arms around Claire's neck.

"I expect your papa will be back soon, shall we go upstairs while we wait for him?"

Mary nodded and then wriggled to get down. Claire lowered her to the ground and Mary scampered off back to the house. A relieved Claire blew out her cheeks.

"Thank you miss," said Fingle, touching a finger to his hat, "she's a nice child, but not a easy one."

Claire gave him a wry smile and followed Mary.

Chapter 6

The Bartons and the Hawksleys returned from their outing and repaired to the drawing room for tea.

"My lord," said Lady Hawksley to Lord Barton, "I believe you have a daughter?"

"Yes, indeed," he replied, "Lady Mary is five years old, nearly six. In a short while I shall bring her down to meet you."

He said a little prayer to himself, hoping Mary was in a good mood after her riding lesson while they had been out. If she was feeling peevish it could be an embarrassing encounter.

A short while later he pushed the nursery door open. Miss Thompson was reading a story with her arm cuddling Mary to her side. It was an endearing picture, which made him feel warm inside and reluctant to disturb the tableau. However, he had guests who were waiting for them downstairs.

"Hello Mary, Miss Thompson."

"Papa!" said Mary, jumping down from the sofa. She ran to her father and threw her arms around his legs. He staggered ever so slightly at the impact.

"Come downstairs with me, our visitors would like to meet you."

Mary frowned. "Don't want to. Miss Thompson is reading me a story."

"She can finish it when you come back."

"I want it now," wailed Mary, stamping her feet and looking up at her father. David's heart sank. He really didn't want to drag a crying, red faced daughter down to the drawing room, but what could he do?

"Mary, Mary," said Claire, coming up behind her. She gently pulled Mary back into an embrace so she could whisper into her ear. "It's only a moment downstairs and on the way, you can tell your papa about all the things you have been doing today. You can tell him how Fingle said you did very well and also, how I thought your riding was wonderfully good. Then you can ask him if you can go riding tomorrow as well. Shall you do that?"

Mary nodded.

"Very good," said Claire, "now come over here a moment while I brush your hair. We want you to look smart and pretty when you go down, don't we?"

As Claire brushed Mary's hair, David was watching them. Her eyes met David's over Mary's head.

"Well done," he mouthed silently. Claire smiled back at him and he returned her smile. His smile gave her a warm feeling, which she ruthlessly suppressed in order to concentrate on Mary's hair.

"There," said Claire to her charge, "you look very nice now." She impulsively kissed Mary on her forehead. "Don't be long now."

"Are you not coming?" Mary asked Claire.

"No, you go with your father. While you are gone I shall look to see what other storybooks you have, ready for when you come back."

Mary hesitated, but only very briefly, before taking her father's hand and heading for the door.

Claire heard Mary's chatter to her father as they headed off down the hallway. She was such an active, busy child, Claire was going to be glad of a few minutes rest. She would be on her way to Lady Sutton tomorrow and she wondered if her ladyship would be more restful. For all she knew, Lady Sutton might have her running upstairs and downstairs all day. At least Lady Mary was a happy child, provided she was kept occupied. Would her ladyship be pleasant company or a cranky, bad tempered old lady? Her engagement letter had not been much of a clue, as it had clearly been written by a secretary. And what would Sutton Hall be like? Somehow she doubted it would as large, elegant and comfortable as Hemingford Park.

Whatever the case, Claire would find out tomorrow.

Chapter 7

A hush descended as they entered the drawing room. Mary had still been chattering to her father, but she fell silent as four pairs of eyes regarded her.

"This is my daughter Lady Mary," said her father, "Mary, make your curtsey to Sir John, Lady Hawksley and Miss Hawksley."

Mary bobbed a rather perfunctory curtsey.

"Oh, isn't she sweet, Felicity," said Lady Hawksley to her daughter.

Mary regarded Lady Hawksley suspiciously.

"Oh yes, absolutely divine," replied Felicity in a colourless voice.

"Come over here, child, and let me see you properly," said Lady Hawksley.

The earl put his hand on Mary's back and gave her a gentle push.

"And how old are you Lady Mary?"

"I'm nearly six."

"I hear you have a new governess."

Mary frowned at Lady Hawksley. "No, she isn't. Miss Thompson is not a governess. She said she wasn't and I like her much better than a governess. She's much, much nicer and I don't like governesses at all."

Lady Hawksley looked over Mary to Lord Barton, with a puzzled expression on her face.

"Did you not say yesterday that Lady Mary was to have a new governess today, my lord?"

He glanced at his mother as he wondered what to say. His mother clearly had no idea. It was unfortunate Lady Hawksley had mentioned a governess in Mary's hearing. He obviously had to find his own way out of this awkward situation.

"It had been our expectation, but there was a delay. Have we had further news?" he asked his mother, as he searched for an explanation to smooth things over. A protesting Lady Mary would not be desirable at this point.

"No, not yet, the groom hasn't returned with any message so far as I am aware. No doubt he will do so quite soon."

This left David still in the dark, not knowing quite what to say, but he had to say something. "In the meantime, Lady Sutton has been kind enough to lend us the services of her companion."

"Lady Sutton?"

"She is the daughter of the old Marquis of Barnstaple," explained Lady Barton, having had time to consult Debrett's Peerage, "she lives in seclusion a few miles to the west of us."

David noticed his mother's vagueness, and didn't himself want to get into further and more complex detail. Certainly not about yesterday's mix up. He didn't think his servant's mistake would reflect well upon them.

"We now suppose the new lady in question will arrive tomorrow, although it has yet to be confirmed."

"Papa, I don't want another governess, I want Miss Thompson instead," said Mary loudly. She was alert enough to realise the 'lady in question' was another unwanted governess, even if her father was avoiding the G word.

"But Lady Mary, you must have a governess, otherwise you won't know how to go on," said Miss Hawksley, smiling sweetly at her.

Mary turned towards her with a mulish expression on her face. David realised the situation could get out of hand at any moment and thus a tactical retreat might be in order.

"Come Mary, it is time for you to return upstairs to Miss Thompson. Say your goodbyes to our guests."

Mary just scowled at everybody, but nevertheless took her father's hand as they left the room.

"I am sure you will be glad to have a governess with firm discipline as soon as possible," commented Sir John, "this Miss Thompson whom you have borrowed obviously has no idea how to deal with a child."

Mary looked angrily back over her shoulder at Sir John, but had no chance to reply before she was jerked out of the room by her father.

"Papa, I don't like those people," said Mary loudly, as they went up the stairs.

"Even if we don't like people, it is important to remain polite," said her father, "if we are rude, everybody gets upset and then it's not nice for anybody."

"I don't like them saying I must have a governess. I don't want a governess."

"Why don't you want a governess?"

"Because they're not nice and smack me if I make a mistake. Sometimes I make mistakes without meaning to, so it's not fair."

"Well, no, I see what you mean. We all make

mistakes sometimes and it's not right to be smacked if it's not deliberate, is it?"

"Do you ever make mistakes, papa?"

"Sometimes I do, but I try hard not to. And I try very hard not to make the same mistake a second time."

"When you were a boy, did you make mistakes?"

"Yes, I did and I would get told off by my parents or my tutor."

"Grandmama told you off?"

"Yes. Even now, she tells me I'm wrong when she thinks I'm making a mistake."

Mary looked up at him thoughtfully as they arrived back at the nursery.

"She doesn't smack your fingers though does she?"

"Oh no, and sometimes it turns out I'm right and she is wrong."

Mary looked up at him in confusion.

"Now and again there isn't a definite right or wrong." They paused outside the nursery. "So, for example, I think you look nicest in the blue dress. But perhaps grandmama thinks you look better in the pink dress, so we don't always agree."

"I like the blue best."

"Why don't we ask Miss Thompson what she thinks?" he said, pushing open the nursery door and hoping for rescue.

Claire paused as they came into the room. She had two books in her hand as she had been going through the books looking for a suitable story.

"My lord?" she asked.

"We were discussing the merits of Lady Mary's

dresses, Miss Thompson. Do you think the pink or the blue suits her best?"

Claire recalled the scene from early morning. "Well, I think the pink is very nice, but I prefer the blue. Possibly there are others in the wardrobe which would be even nicer."

"See?" said Mary, triumphantly, "we are right and grandmama is wrong."

"Yes, perhaps so," said her father, "but we don't need to tell her, do we? She might worry we'll smack her fingers, mightn't she?"

Mary giggled at the absurdity of the notion. David and Claire smiled at each other.

He was relieved his daughter's good humour was restored. "Thank you Miss Thompson, I shall return to our visitors and leave Lady Mary in your care."

As he headed back downstairs, he was relieved to have left Mary in capable hands. He also reflected that Miss Thompson was a very attractive young lady and was actually more eligible than Miss Hawksley, being the daughter of a baron rather than a baronet. However, she was still a servant and it was unwise to dwell upon the charms of servants. Besides, he kept telling himself, she would be gone far away tomorrow. Then he thought about the discussion with Mary about mistakes and his confession he still made them now and again. He wondered if Miss Hawksley was a potential mistake and one which he should take care to avoid.

Chapter 8

The following morning, David was in his study, attending to paperwork before his visitors arose for the day. There was a knock on the door and Blake entered with a letter on a silver salver.

"The groom has only just returned with this letter sir. He apologises for the delay, but Lady Sutton was not at home when he arrived and he was obliged to wait until late in the evening before she returned."

David took the letter and broke the wax seal. He scanned the letter quickly whilst Blake waited to see if he was required further.

"What!" exclaimed David, looking up in amazement. Blake remained impassive. David bent his head and read the letter again, in case he had misunderstood.

"Oh, this is unbelievable, insupportable," he said and thumped the desk with his fist. "Blake, ask Miss Thompson, no, no, not Miss Thompson, ask the dowager to attend me as soon as possible."

"At once, sir," said Blake, walking towards the door in a measured manner, which passed for haste in a butler such as him.

David rose to his feet, throwing the letter down to the desk as he did so. He paced angrily up and down his study with his hands clasped behind his back, as he waited for his mother.

The dowager came into the room and stopped suddenly as she saw how he was agitated.

"Barton, what is it?"

"Lady Sutton, the sheer effrontery of the woman! She is impudent and uncivil. She has stolen our governess."

"Stolen our governess? What on earth can you mean?"

"Here," he said, taking the letter from his desk and handing it to her, "it seems that an older Miss Thompson suits her ladyship very well. She has offered her the post of companion, as the younger Miss Thompson did not appear. It would seem the older Miss Thompson has accepted the post, so now Lady Sutton refuses to exchange them. Presumably the older Miss Thompson has been offered more money for fewer duties."

"What an abominable woman. How dare she do such a thing?" asked his mother.

"You mean Lady Sutton or the other Miss Thompson?"

"Either. Both."

"It leaves us in bit of a fix," said David.

"What are we going to tell the Hawksleys?" asked the dowager.

"The Hawksleys? Nothing. If they ask, we shall say there is a further delay. There definitely will be a delay because I must write to the agency. In fact I shall write a very blunt letter to the agency and tell them any further candidates must come here for an interview. Furthermore, the agency can pay the travelling costs of sending them. It will give the agency an additional incentive to send someone suitable."

"I expect the Hawksleys will invite us for a return

visit. We have to put them off until we have appointed the governess."

"No, we will decline their invitation," said David.

"Decline? What about Miss Felicity?"

He waved dismissively. "I have thought about it and she does not suit. She is an empty-headed nincompoop. She would drive me to distraction within a month."

"She is very beautiful and very suitable. You need not see much of her after the marriage."

"It is entirely beside the point. Whoever I marry must at least be capable of intelligent conversation. I don't know where you found her, but wherever it was, she can go back there. It was through one of your acquaintances I suppose."

"You are being very harsh on the poor girl," said the dowager with a frown.

"Well I am very sorry, but Lady Sutton has put me in a foul mood." He drummed his fingers on the desktop. "Speaking of poor girls, what are we to do with the young Miss Thompson?"

"We have to keep her, at least for the moment until the Hawksleys have gone. We certainly can't send her off to Lady Sutton now. I mean, what else can we do?" said the dowager.

David reflected on the situation for a minute or so, while his mother waited patiently. He thought there might be a better approach.

"I think, perhaps when the Hawksleys have gone, we should all go to London for a week or so. It would speed up and simplify finding a new governess and be a convenient excuse too, for not visiting the Hawksleys."

"They may just decide to go to London too."

"It can't be helped. If they're not in the same house as us it's easier to pay Miss Hawksley no particular attention. Let us find out first if Miss Thompson is willing to continue as companion to Mary."

David rang the bell. Blake appeared instantly, obviously having waited just outside in anticipation of such a call.

"Blake, ask Miss Thompson to join us if you please. Oh, and my secretary too."

As on the day before, Claire was breakfasting when Blake approached her. She expected the guests to rise somewhat later, giving her time to eat first. Like this she had more choice of the dishes, rather than simply getting a tray in her room. She had left Mary to the care of her nursemaid.

"Miss Thompson," he said, "Lord and Lady Barton ask you to join them in the study as soon as convenient."

Claire correctly interpreted 'as soon as convenient' as 'right now if you can manage it'. She quickly finished her coffee and stood as Blake pulled out her chair. Well, this was, after all, what she had expected. She had not fully unpacked her valise in anticipation of travelling to Lady Sutton today. No doubt the carriage would be at the door shortly, so she wouldn't have much time to pack her bag again and then say goodbye to Lady Mary. She followed Blake to the earl's study.

"Miss Thompson," Blake announced, before closing the door behind her. She went down the room to where the armchairs were ranged in front of the big window.

"Miss Thompson, please take a seat," said David, standing. "Unfortunately, a complication has arisen," he said, resuming his place once she was seated. "I had a letter from Lady Sutton this morning. In it she says that she has made the other Miss Thompson her companion in your place. Naturally we are very angry she has done this, as it is entirely self-serving of both of them. However, it means you don't have the post you expected and we don't have the governess we expected."

Claire stared at him in shock. It was devastating news. She gripped her hands tightly in her lap and willed herself to remain calm. Tears would be pointless, she thought. She had been abandoned, with no prospects, and in a part of the country unfamiliar to her. She would have to go home and it would be utterly humiliating. She hoped her father wouldn't blame her for the mistake in Stony Stratford. At least the countess had said they would pay the stagecoach fare and as well she would have a little money to take with her. It seems a carriage at the front door would be taking her only as far as Stony Stratford, not to Sutton Hall. At least there were so many stagecoaches passing through the town it shouldn't be hard to get a seat. She wondered how long it was going to take to find another post?

"Miss Thompson, I realise this must be a shock," said the dowager, interrupting Claire's dismal thoughts, "but please try not to be downhearted. We are not going to simply cast you off. Indeed we would be grateful if you would agree to stay for a few days more."

Claire looked up. A few days more? She could do this. It would give her time to plan ahead and to earn a little more as well. She liked Lady Mary, even if she was a little tiresome and bad tempered now and again. Claire saw she should write to her father too, so he knew what had happened. Then he wouldn't be too shocked if she suddenly turned up on his doorstep. She nodded agreement, unsure what to say.

"In a few days," said the earl, "we think to remove to London for a week or so. That is to say Lady Barton, myself and Lady Mary. We would like you to come with us too. Is that agreeable?"

"Yes sir, I shall be happy to do so," said Claire. This was even better, she thought. She could get home in less than a day on the stagecoach from London. She could also visit agencies in London to look for a new post, which would be much quicker than writing to them and, who knows, she might not even need to go home. Yes, this was definitely an arrangement which suited her.

"My secretary, Mr Trevor," he indicated a smart young man standing quietly near the desk, "will be writing to the agency, explaining our displeasure at the action of the elder Miss Thompson. He will be asking them to make a new shortlist of governesses for us to see in London. If you give him the details, he will also write to your own agency and explain why you have not taken up the post with Lady Sutton, due to no fault of your own."

Claire was pleased to hear this, as it would definitely accelerate the process of finding another post and also mean her reputation would remain unblemished.

"Thank you sir, if Mr Trevor would come up to the nursery, I will give him the name and direction."

"Very good. I find our visitors are not interested in horses, so you may feel free to take Lady Mary down to the stables for her lesson this afternoon. As for this morning, I leave her activities to your discretion."

"Thank you my lord," said Claire, smiling with relief. "Before I go to Lady Mary, may I write a short letter to my father so he knows where I am?"

"Of course. I assume you have writing materials in your room. If not, ask Mr Trevor. I shall write a short note of my own to your father as well, apologising for taking advantage of your goodwill in this fashion. If I pass it to you, perhaps you could enclose it within your letter? Then if you hand it my secretary, I will frank it for you before it is posted."

Claire curtsied and left the study.

David blew out his cheeks. This was half of the problem resolved. Miss Thompson appeared to have managed fairly well yesterday and hopefully she would continue to manage Mary until they arrived in London.

"What shall we do with the Hawksleys today?" he asked his mother.

"I had thought to show them around the house. However, if you are quite sure you won't suit, I can't do it, otherwise they are liable to get the wrong idea."

"No, quite so. I shall ask Sir John if he would like

to go shooting with me or play billiards if not. This will keep me away from Miss Hawksley. At the same time, I will mention my pressing and urgent business in London next week, which has just arisen in this morning's post. This should forestall any return invitation. Hopefully he will also take it as a hint I will not be making any offer for his daughter. If you could show the ladies our gardens or the succession houses or something? "

Claire slowly made her way up to the nursery while she considered what to do. Firstly she should write to her father. Then, secondly, perhaps she should try to get Lady Mary to do a little schoolwork. She felt vaguely guilty Lady Mary wasn't being taught anything, which could be considered at least partly Claire's fault. She stopped at the nursery. Maisie was helping Mary with her breakfast of boiled egg and buttered bread.

"Good morning, Lady Mary, I am going to write a letter to my papa while you finish your breakfast and then I will be back."

Mary looked briefly at Claire, before continuing to give her full attention to the egg.

The letter written, the earl's note enclosed and the whole thing sent down to the secretary, Claire returned to the nursery.

"Miss Thompson," said Mary, "when are you leaving?"

Claire was taken aback. If Mary wanted her to go away, the situation was even more complicated.

"Your papa asked me if I could stay a little

longer. He said you're all going to London in a few days and I could go with you."

Mary looked thoughtfully at Claire while she considered this new information.

"You said you were leaving today. Are you quite sure you're not a governess?"

"Quite, quite sure."

"Then why aren't you leaving today?"

Claire could see Mary was both clever and thoughtful. She had remembered what had been said, and now the plan had changed, she was once again suspicious of being tricked into having another governess. Claire could see more explanation was needed.

"I was supposed to go and be a companion to an old lady, but because I didn't arrive when I was supposed to, she has found someone else instead to take my place. Now I have to go back home and it's not very nice on the stagecoach. Your papa said he needs to go to London with you and your grandmama and because London is half way to my home, your papa said I could go with you, instead of on the stagecoach."

This was an edited and simplified version of the situation, but Claire definitely didn't want to talk about plans involving governesses.

Mary mulled this over and then a mulish expression appeared on her face.

"I don't want to go to London. I want to stay here and ride Moonbeam."

Mary pressed her lips together, crossed her arms and looked belligerently at Claire. Claire realised this was an argument she didn't want to have. Going to

London wasn't her idea and besides, it wasn't Claire, it was the earl, who needed to tell Mary they were going. At least Mary wasn't still talking about her leaving today. Perhaps Mary didn't mind if Claire stayed a little longer. However, there could be an argument when next Mary saw the earl and the removal to London was discussed. Claire thought it would be wise, and to her own benefit, if she could defuse the situation a little in advance and deflect this obsession with Moonbeam.

"When you are in London you could go to Astley's Amphitheatre."

"What's ashleys … what you said?"

"It's a show where people do all sorts of amazing things on horses."

"Horses?" Mary's face brightened. "What sorts of things?"

"Well, there are girls who ride standing up on the horse, or ride two horses at once." Claire was a bit vague about the details, having only received her limited information at second hand.

"Really? What else do they do?"

"I don't know, I've never been, I've only been told about it by other people. I think they said there were clowns and acrobats too."

"Yes, I want to go and you can come with me!" said Mary, looking pleased with herself.

"I don't know if I can. I might have gone home by then. We'll have to see what your papa says." Claire didn't want to make promises she was unlikely to keep, although she really would like to go if the opportunity arose. However, as long as the earl took his daughter, it wouldn't matter if Claire was there or not. She must remember to suggest the idea to his lordship.

"Where is papa?"

"The last time I saw him he was with grandmama and Mr Trevor, but I expect he has gone somewhere with the visitors by now. I expect he will come and see you later, like he did yesterday."

Mary considered the matter for a few moments, before clearly dismissing it.

"What shall we do today, Miss Thompson?"

Claire was relieved they had moved on from her imminent departure and the proposed journey to London. She wondered how she could gently introduce something educational without instigating an anti-governess tirade.

"Yesterday, I read you a story. Why don't you read one to me today?"

Mary's face darkened again.

"I don't want to. I'll make mistakes and you'll get cross and shout at me."

"No, I promise I won't get cross and I definitely won't shout at you. I'll help you with the difficult bits. I'm sure I saw some books yesterday which didn't look very hard. Let me show them to you and you can see if you want to do it or not."

David and Sir John finished their third game of billiards.

"Thank you for the games," said Sir John, putting his cue back in the rack. "I nearly had you in the last one. If you'll excuse me now, I'll go and freshen up before luncheon."

"Yes, thank you. I must say the last game was

very close," said David, "I will see you shortly."

David had enjoyed the games, but not because Sir John was a challenging player. He had realised after the first game that his guest was a very indifferent player. No, the challenge was to make Sir John win the second game and only just lose the third game, without him knowing David was deliberately arranging it. It had been the polite thing to do and an interesting objective too.

There had been no exasperating visits from his daughter or her companion, so he was curious to see what they had been doing all morning. When he arrived at the nursery, he found Mary and Claire sitting on the sofa, engrossed in a book open on Mary's lap. As he entered the room, Mary noticed him and sprang to her feet, knocking the book to the floor, and ran to him.

"Papa, papa, I've been reading a book, come with me and I will read it to you," she grabbed his hand and pulled him to the sofa.

Claire picked up the book and moved to the end of the sofa to make space.

David was thoroughly bemused. Never before had Mary offered to read to him. In fact, he couldn't recall her reading a book before, although he had assumed the governess would have been teaching Mary to read. He glanced, with raised eyebrows, at Claire, who appeared to be suppressing a grin.

Mary sat next to Claire and David sat on the other side of Mary. Mary took the book from Claire and opened it to the first page.

"What's the book called?" asked David.

"It's called My Pretty Pony," said Mary, "Miss

Thompson found it on the shelf. She's very clever 'cos I didn't even know it was there."

David looked a question at Claire over Mary's head. Claire just shrugged. David wondered why his pony mad daughter had not known the book was there. He hadn't bought it himself and he wondered who had done so? Presumably someone else in the family. He would have to ask his mother about it. In any case, the governess had obviously not used it. Had she thought the book unsuitable? There were a lot of questions he should have been asking, but hadn't. Had grief over his wife's death let him get into a habit of ignoring his daughter?

"It sounds very interesting," he said, "will you read it to me please?"

Mary started to read it quite slowly and hesitantly. Now and again, when she paused, Claire whispered in her ear and then Mary would carry on. It wasn't a very long story, as it was a first reading book without many words. When Mary got to the end, she looked triumphantly at her father.

"Oh, Mary, you did very well," he said, "I'm so proud of you and I shall tell grandmama how good you are at reading."

"Miss Thompson helped me a little," confessed Mary. "I like Miss Thompson, she's nice and don't smack my fingers if I get stuck." Mary rested her head against Claire's arm.

David smiled at Claire, who gave the impression of being slightly embarrassed at this show of affection by Mary. Like Mary, he liked Miss Thompson and thought she was nice too.

"My lord," said Claire, snapping him out of his

musings as he smiled at her, "Lady Mary was not at all happy to be going to London. She said she wanted to stay here so she could ride her pony. However, I said if she went to London, then you might have time to take her to Astley's Amphitheatre where she could see people doing clever things on horses."

David was a little caught off balance. He hadn't given much thought yet as to what they would do in London. He had vaguely expected to be very busy with business matters and finding a new governess. It had certainly not occurred to him to take Mary to the show. He noticed Mary looking up at him earnestly. Claire was staring at him too and nodding her head ever so slightly. Ah. So there was a message there and if he wasn't mistaken, he was being urged to agree. More than likely to avoid fraught and tearful scenes. He could, no doubt, make time for it and, after all, there was little reason for not going, was there? It might be fun to take his horse mad daughter to the show, and they hadn't done much together had they?

"Very well, we shall do so," he said, "but now I must go down for luncheon with our guests. I shall see you later."

He had been sure this morning that not offering for Miss Hawksley and instead gently sending her and her parents home had been the right decision. Now, broad smiles on both Mary and Miss Thompson made him feel absurdly pleased at having done something else right as well.

Chapter 9

Claire and Mary were descending the main staircase after lunch and a nap, on their way to the stables. Claire heard voices in the entrance hall.

"Lady Mary, wait!" she said, mindful they were supposed to be keeping clear of the visitors. Mary paid no attention, and continued downstairs, being too eager for her riding lesson. Claire had a dilemma. If she raised her voice to halt Mary, the visitors would hear her. If she didn't they would be upon them in moments. As she hesitated, she realised it was too late anyway. Mary reached the ground floor, glanced at the visitors and simply scampered past.

"Mary!" said the dowager, but to no avail. Mary had already reached a turn in the hallway and disappeared from sight.

Claire reached the ground floor too to find all the visitors and the dowager looking at her with disapproval on their faces. She curtsied hurriedly, vaguely in the direction of the group.

"I beg your pardon milady," she said to the dowager before disappearing in pursuit of Mary.

"And who, precisely, was that?" said Lady Hawksley in icy tones.

"Lady Sutton's companion, whom we have borrowed to bear Lady Mary company until her governess arrives," said the dowager with a sigh.

"I sure you will agree, Lady Barton," said Sir John, "the sooner the governess arrives, the better.

This companion of Lady Sutton obviously has no control over the child."

The earl arrived in the entrance hall. "My apologies for keeping you waiting," he said, "my thanks for your company and perhaps we shall see you all in London during the season?"

"Indeed," said Sir John shaking his hand, "our thanks for your hospitality. Now come along ladies, we mustn't keep the horses standing."

David and his mother stood on the top step, watching the Hawksleys climb into their carriage.

"They didn't make a fuss about leaving early," remarked the dowager quietly.

"No, I dropped some hints to Sir John while we were playing billiards. He understood immediately there was no point in them hanging around. He is an able politician and quickly thought of a reason why they should be elsewhere."

As the carriage moved away, they heard footsteps inside the doorway behind them and a discreet cough. They both turned around to see who was there.

"Mary!" shouted Claire as she exited the house in the Mary's wake. "Mary wait!"

Mary stopped on the path and turned to see what Claire wanted.

"Mary, that was not well done," gasped a slightly breathless Claire. "It was very rude to run past everybody like that without a greeting or a curtsey or anything."

"I don't like them. Especially the young one, even

if she is going to be my new mother."

She crossed her arms and scowled at Claire.

"Your new mother?"

"Yes, Maisie said papa was going to marry her and then she would be my new mother. I don't want him to marry her because I don't like her."

"I think Maisie says too much. Anyway, it looked as if they were leaving, so Maisie might be wrong. In any case, it's not nice to be rude to people, otherwise they won't be nice to you either, will they?"

"Are you going to smack me?"

"No! I'm not going to smack you. Absolutely not. I'm going to ask you to go back and say sorry to your grandmama for being rude to everybody."

"Shan't," said Mary, pouting.

"Very well, I shall go and tell Fingle your riding lesson is cancelled."

"No!" wailed Mary, stamping her foot, "you can't do that."

"Oh yes I can. You have a choice. Apologise to grandmama and then have your lesson with Moonbeam and Fingle. Or, don't apologise and don't have your lesson. It's entirely up to you."

"My papa said I could have my lesson, so I can and you can't stop me," said Mary mutinously.

"I think your papa might be cross with you at the moment for being rude to his guests, so he might have just changed his mind."

Mary stared at Claire belligerently, but Claire just stared back at her. Then Mary sighed, and sagged, and turned back towards the house. Claire offered her hand and, after a slight hesitation, Mary took it.

"When we get there, say 'Grandmama I'm sorry I

was rude before'" said Claire quietly as they approached the side door.

They arrived back in the entrance hall to see the dowager and the earl standing in the doorway, waving goodbye to their visitors.

Claire coughed gently to attract their attention and they turned around. She softly squeezed Mary's hand.

"Grandmama, I'm sorry I was rude before," said Mary.

The dowager blinked with surprise.

"I'm glad to hear it Mary," she said, "it was not well done. However, I accept your apology and we shall not speak of it again."

"Miss Thompson," said Mary, looking up, "may I have my riding lesson now?"

"With your permission?" asked Claire of the earl and dowager.

"Yes, you may, run along," said the countess.

David and his mother watched them depart.

"Miss Thompson seems to have had a beneficial effect on Mary in a very short space of time," said the countess.

"Yes, indeed. Every time I have gone up to the nursery the atmosphere seems so much better than before. I have a feeling there may be a great deal I did not understand previously. I believe I might have a chat with Miss Thompson while Mary is having her riding lesson," he said, before following them to the stables.

The countess watched him go, before making her way slowly and thoughtfully to her sitting room.

Chapter 10

David arrived at the paddock just as Fingle led Mary and Moonbeam through the gate. Claire glanced around as she heard his footsteps approaching. He joined Claire at the rail, and they watched horse and rider for a few moments.

"Miss Thompson, her ladyship and I think you have done remarkably well with Mary in a very short space of time."

"Thank you sir, but I must apologise for the incident just now. It had not occurred to me how everybody might be waiting in the entrance hall. Had I known we could easily have gone a little later."

"It's of no matter," he said, waving his hand dismissively, "but now they have gone, there is no need to hide yourself and Mary away. You may feel free to move about as it suits you. Their visit was an awkward business and I'm glad there is an end to it."

"Will they be returning again before you leave for London?"

"No, definitely not."

Claire looked at him thoughtfully as he watched Mary on her pony. Claire wondered if, from his emphatic tone, the betrothal which had been expected by the servants was not going to happen. Or at least, not just yet. Perhaps it would progress further in London. She didn't know Miss Hawksley, but for some obscure reason she liked the idea of the earl being free of the attachment.

He turned to look at her, noticing her scrutiny from the corner of his eye.

"Miss Thompson, is it your experience of younger siblings which has enabled you to deal with Lady Mary so effectively?"

"Possibly so. However, and I don't wish to be impertinent, I have the impression her recent governess must have been a rather severe lady. Lady Mary now has the opinion that all governesses are harsh and unpleasant."

"Perhaps she was harsh because Mary was misbehaving a great deal."

"I think Mary was simply craving attention. Misbehaving might have been a way to get attention, even if it was painful."

"Ah. I consider myself reprimanded."

"Oh, I beg your pardon, I didn't mean...."

"No, no, you are perfectly correct. I see now, some time ago I had become too engrossed in my own grief to spend enough time with my daughter. After a while it probably became a habit and persisted even though the grief has since faded. Sometimes it takes someone from outside to be able to stand back and see the situation for what it is. I thank you for being frank with me and not being afraid to point it out. Perhaps it helps that you are not really an employee?"

Claire opened her mouth to speak, realised she didn't know what to say, and promptly shut it again.

"Speaking of which, Miss Thompson, our visitors have departed, Mary seems happier, and there is no case now for awkward situations and consequent explanations. I will still appreciate you spending time with Mary and as well, will endeavour now to join you both whenever I can. Perhaps Mary could spend time with her grandmother too. I will still compensate you for your efforts, but otherwise, please consider yourself a guest and join us for dinner in future. Perhaps you should move to a guest room as well, instead of being on the nursery floor. I will tell her ladyship to expect you for dinner, for her to spend time with Mary and why this should be."

"Thank you, my lord, but I am perfectly happy with a tray in my room and please don't move me to a guest room. It is very convenient to be in a room near the nursery."

"Very well, stay in your current room, we will be moving to London very shortly in any case. However, please do join us for dinner. We will appreciate your company and besides, it will be less work for the servants."

Claire didn't think the servants were especially bothered by giving her dinner on a tray in her room, but it was a good excuse. However, as she was now staying here longer, it seemed she needed to unpack everything from her valise. She would have to make sure her best evening dress wasn't creased. If it was, would it be in order for her to ask for a maid to iron it? She hoped she wouldn't be expected to iron it herself. She knew from past experience this would be a recipe for disaster. She would have to ask Mrs Newsome discreetly. Since Claire's status in the household was a bit hazy, it was difficult to know if it would be an acceptable request or not. If necessary, she would have to beg a favour of her.

"Thank you my lord, in that case I will join you for dinner."

"Perhaps, since you are now a guest, you should

also call me 'Barton' instead of 'my lord'?" he said, with a raised eyebrow.

Claire flushed slightly. She wasn't at all sure about this, she still felt like a servant, rather than a guest. Calling him 'Barton' was getting much, much too personal. She didn't know how to reply, so she didn't and simply gave her attention back to Mary, who was circling the paddock on her pony. Mary noticed them looking and waved. Both David and Claire waved back.

Chapter 11

Claire looked at herself in the mirror. She was wearing a grey silk gown which fitted her well. She had packed it very carefully and the only creases were tiny and easy to overlook. As she had anticipated becoming a companion to the daughter of a marquess, she had brought her two best evening gowns from home. Her other, more worn, gowns she had bequeathed to her younger sister to take apart and reuse the material as best she could. The two she had brought were sadly out of date and a bit plain, but they were otherwise in good condition and all she had for evening wear. Never mind, it was only the earl and his mother and she was not expected to cut a dash, was she? She added her only jewellery, a string of pearls, and headed down to the drawing room, where Blake offered her a sherry.

Lord Barton and his mother were already there. His mother looked Claire over and seemed to approve .

"We were discussing Mary and wondered if you had any plans for her tomorrow?" said David.

"I have no firm ideas, but if you don't mind, I should be pleased to go around the garden with her at some point. I expect the grass will be dry by then."

"I shall be happy to show you around, perhaps in mid morning?" said the dowager.

"Thank you my lady, if you would send a maid for us when it is convenient, I'm sure we'll find something useful to do in the meantime."

"Dinner is served, my lord," announced Blake.

77

"Dinner will be served in the small dining room," David explained to Claire, as they followed the countess, "the large dining room will accommodate twenty people, but it's inconvenient when there are only a handful of us."

Once the soup course had been removed, Claire turned to the earl.

"My lord, I am grateful to be going to London with you, as it will make it easier for me to find a fresh post. I understand you would like me to spend time with Lady Mary until you find a suitable governess. However, in London, I would be obliged if you could spare me from time to time so I may visit the employment agencies."

"Of course you may. We remain grateful for your assistance for as long as you are able to do so," said David, "moreover, since you have a good rapport with Mary, I am hoping you will be able to assist me in selecting a suitable governess. As well, I imagine we will have to refer to said governess as a tutor, rather than a governess, if we are to gain Mary's cooperation."

"I have a much better idea," said the countess, and the other two looked at her with a little surprise, wondering what she was thinking of.

"I have it in mind to attend the theatre and perhaps the opera too, while we are in town." She turned to speak to Claire, "I know my son does not care for opera and only goes at my insistence."

David nodded guiltily.

"I propose therefore, Miss Thompson, making you my companion from the time we arrive in Half

Moon Street. This way we kill several birds with one stone. Mary need not lose someone she has become attached to whilst a new governess is introduced. Your presence in the house doesn't then cause confusion amongst the servants. I have company around town. Barton is free from dancing attendance on me to conduct his business or visit his clubs or do whatever is necessary. Finally there is no need for you, Miss Thompson to go trudging around agencies, at least for several weeks. What do you think of that?"

Claire thought this was a wonderful idea. She liked this family and the proposal wiped away all uncertainty about her future, at least for several weeks. Furthermore she would dearly love to go to the theatre and the opera in London. She wasn't sure how long was 'several', but it had to be at least two or three before she needed to go around the agencies. Then, if Mr Trevor had written to them on her behalf, they might simply let her know when there was a suitable position without her needing to trudge around town. A letter from the secretary of an earl probably counted as a recommendation too, especially when the agencies realised she was staying with the dowager countess as her companion.

"Thank you milady, it will suit me very well and simplify many things. I shall write to my father tomorrow and tell him of the change of plan, as he will be worrying about what will become of me."

The dowager was revising her ideas about Miss Thompson. She seemed like a sensible girl, not like the featherbrained Miss Hawksley, and had apparently endeared herself to Lady Mary. Her manner was modest, very acceptable and she seemed to know how to behave in company. Miss Thompson's conduct this evening had been everything the dowager could expect in a well brought-up girl. She was also, if anything, more eligible than Miss Hawksley, being the daughter of a baron rather than a baronet, except, of course, she was penniless. However, the very likely lack of a dowry need not matter, since the Barton Earldom was comfortably prosperous. And it was past time David re-married. The dowager thought to keep Miss Thompson around a little longer, as she did appear to be a distinct possibility as the next Countess Barton.

More to the point, Miss Thompson and her son were no more than polite and civil to each other as far as the dowager could see, which wasn't very promising. It would be interesting to see what would happen when they were thrown into each other's company a little more. David might not care for opera, but he would definitely be joining them at the theatre, although he didn't realise it just yet. With a bit of luck, there would be a ball or musicale or some other event as well, for which she, and Miss Thompson, would require his escort. It would be easier too if Miss Thompson was promoted to companion instead of not-governess.

As another course was being served, the dowager glanced from her son to a potential daughter-in-law and back again. And, yes, there was definitely a distinct possibility here, but regardless, they might have no interest in each other. And if nothing happened in the next couple of weeks except the acquisition of a new governess, then, yes, the family could simply return to the country. Miss Thompson could be given a generous gift and wished adieu. The countess allowed herself a little feeling of satisfaction at her plan and applied herself to her plate.

Chapter 12 - Monday

They arrived in Half Moon Street very late in the day. Mary was carried up to bed by Maisie and everybody else went to their rooms to change for dinner. Claire had been given a room next to the dowager, as befitted her ladyship's companion. Claire was very happy with her room, it was bigger than anything at home, and luxuriously furnished. Her feet sank into a thick rug and all the soft furnishings had a pink floral theme on a light cream background. She couldn't resist going to the bed and trying it. It was as soft as it looked.

However, as she lay there, looking up at the canopy above, she recognised she wasn't clear how long her stay would last. Lady Barton had said she wanted company while she was in town, but inevitably the family would all be going back to Hemingford Park at some point, perhaps in two or three weeks. Claire remembered when they had first met, Lady Barton had been quite emphatic to the earl that she hadn't engaged a companion, because she didn't need one. So when they returned, would Claire be going with her? Almost certainly not. This was just a temporary convenience for all concerned. When Lady Barton had made Claire her companion, how long it would last hadn't been clear and Claire hadn't thought to ask for more detail. Perhaps she should have done so. The vagueness was confusing. Even in subsequent conversations, Lady Barton hadn't said anything at all about what would happen when they returned from London to the country, nor when it would be.

Never mind, she thought, she would enjoy it while she could. More than likely, it all depended on how long it would take to find a suitable governess. Perhaps when they left for Hemingford Park, they would let her stay another couple of days in Half Moon Street while she found a new post. Failing which, she could always get home in less than a day from here. In the meantime, she had to take care not to fall asleep, but get changed. As she climbed down from the high bed, there was a tap at the door and a maid came in.

"Good evening miss," she said, "my name is Sally and I'll be acting as your lady's maid while you are here." Sally deposited a jug of hot water on the washstand in the corner.

Claire was astounded. She merited a lady's maid? Her astonishment obviously showed on her face.

"I'm usually a chambermaid, but Robbins, her ladyship's maid, said she would help me if there was something I didn't know."

There was a noise in the corridor and Sally opened the door to retrieve Claire's baggage.

Claire gathered her wits about her again. She need to get changed without more delay.

"Very well, Sally, there is a grey silk in the bag for now. Hopefully it has not become creased."

When Claire went down for the pre-dinner drinks, the dowager was there, but the earl had yet to arrive. Lady Barton studied Claire's grey silk evening dress thoughtfully.

"Miss Thompson, tomorrow morning you and I

need to visit the modiste."

"Oh. Should I not be staying here in the nursery with Lady Mary?"

"Her nursemaid can take care of her for a few hours. In any case, if you don't go to the modiste, how shall she fit you for new evening and day dresses?" said Lady Barton with an amused smile.

"Dresses for me? But I ..." This was not something Claire had considered.

"Yes, yes, Miss Thompson, for you. The dresses you have been wearing are fine for the country or when we have no visitors, but if you are to go around with me, you really must have something rather more fashionable and stylish."

"Oh. I see," said Claire, blinking with surprise. She knew her dresses were sadly provincial and somewhat out of date too, but she had given no thought to anything new. Especially if it was only for a week or two. Besides, she had no money.

"Obviously I will pay for it, since we both know you couldn't possibly afford it."

This was true, and merely echoing Claire's own thoughts, but she didn't really need it to be said in such blunt terms. She still had a little pride. However, she supposed she had to accept this as her reality now. In a way, it was like one of the maids being provided with a uniform, wasn't it?

"And while we are there," continued Lady Barton, "you will need a theatre gown, a carriage gown and possibly a ball gown too."

"A ball gown?" Claire hadn't considered the possibility of attending any balls. Why would Lady Barton want to attend a ball? Surely she didn't dance?

"Oh yes, we might as well cater for all possibilities. Who knows where we might be invited or for how long we shall be here?"

Claire was completely flummoxed. This was not at all what she had expected. She had thought they might go out a couple of times in the evening and a few times in the day with Lady Mary.
However, this was starting to sound like a full-blown social whirl. A suspicious thought crept into her mind, of Lady Barton planning to do a little matchmaking, as compensation for disrupting Claire's plans of a quiet life with Lady Sutton, somewhere deep in Buckinghamshire. But no, this would be entirely out of proportion, it was more likely Lady Barton planned to stay a little longer in London than Claire had supposed. There was no reason her ladyship couldn't do so, when she had a companion with her. And her ladyship could stay even if Lady Mary, her father and her new governess went back to Hemingford Park in the meantime. Was this the main reason behind Lady Barton wanting a companion for a while? If this were the case, it suited Claire. Anyway, she would find out soon enough, and it was a long time since she had new dresses.

Just then, the earl arrived in the salon.

"My lord," said Claire, "when do you propose to take Lady Mary to Astley's? She is sure to ask me tomorrow."

"Is tomorrow too soon?" he said.

"Oh yes, much too soon," said the countess,

"Miss Thompson can't possibly go out in public until she has a new day dress."

"But milady, surely I don't need to go to Astley's with Lady Mary and my lord?"

"Oh, but you must. Barton will need someone to assist with Mary. We can't send Mary's nursemaid, otherwise it would cause resentment amongst the other servants. I am certainly not going, I don't care for that sort of entertainment. Besides, it was your idea, was it not? No, it must be you Miss Thompson."

"Should we not take a maid as chaperone?"

"Chaperone? I think a five year old girl will serve perfectly well as a chaperone."

Claire couldn't quite see the logic to all these arguments, but she could see opposition was futile. Lady Barton clearly had her mind set on how things would be and wasn't open to alternatives. Besides, in Claire's position, she needed to do as she was told. Even so, it was all slightly bewildering.

Chapter13 - Tuesday

"Miss Thompson, what shall we do today?" asked Mary, as soon as she had finished her breakfast.

"This morning your grandmama is taking me to the dressmaker to get some new dresses made, so I will have to leave you with Maisie. I'm sure the two of you will think of something."

"Can I come with you and grandmama?"

"I don't think you will find it very interesting. Most of the time I will just be standing around while they measure me or we look at dress patterns. When they deliver the new dresses you can come to my room and have a look at them all with me. How about that?"

Mary nodded.

"Shall we read a book while we wait for grandmama to get ready and for the carriage to be brought around?"

After a couple of hours at the modiste, Claire was taken to have new slippers, shoes and boots made, then for gloves and bonnets. The dowager appeared to be comprehensively enjoying herself. By the time they returned to Half Moon Street for a late luncheon, Claire was exhausted. After the meal, she was glad the dowager went to her room for a rest and Lady Mary was also napping. Claire decided this was an excellent plan and went for a nap herself.

After a short, but refreshing twenty minutes, Claire went in search of Mary.

"Lady Mary, would you like to go for a walk in the park?" asked Claire.

"Are there horses in the park?"

Claire could see this obsession with horses might prove annoying, but Claire really wanted to get out of the house, go for a walk and get some fresh air. Or at least, what passed for fresh air in London. She missed her frequent walks in the countryside at home.

"I don't think so, but my maid Sally says there is a pond with a fountain and ducks."

"Ducks?" said Mary dubiously, weighing the up the attractions of ducks. She had a picture book with ducks in it, but there were no ducks at Hemingford Park. Not as far as Claire had seen in her limited time there anyway.

"What do you do with ducks?"

"We could ask cook for some bread for you to throw to the ducks."

"Do they like bread?"

"Oh yes, and they race each other to get the bits of bread and do a lot of excited quacking when they see you throwing the bread for them."

"Are they fierce?"

"Fierce? They may be noisy and flap their wings a lot when they're trying to get the bread before the other ducks get it, but no, they're not fierce."

"Is the park far away?"

"Oh no, Green Park is at the end of the street, it will only take us a moment to walk there.

"Alright, lets go," said Mary, "and then perhaps afterwards we can go and see some horses."

Claire sighed.

"We shall see if there is enough time this afternoon and later on ask your papa about horses. We might have to go and see horses tomorrow instead of today if there isn't enough time. For now, let Maisie put your boots and cloak on before taking you downstairs. I shall get dressed as well and see you in the entrance hall after asking cook for some bread."

A short while later Claire and Mary were in the hall with a footman carrying a cloth bag containing stale bread. Claire had tried to dispense with the footman. After all, anybody observing them would probably think she was the governess or nursemaid who wouldn't warrant the escort of a footman. Especially if, as the dowager had said, she wasn't wearing anything fashionable, but instead a plain dress fit for the countryside. However, Ives, the London butler, insisted the footman go too, conscious of how Claire was a companion, almost a guest, and not merely a servant. He reminded her they were now in London, not in the country, and said the footman had nothing better to do anyway. Claire gave in, since she thought the footman almost certainly knew the area, which Claire didn't, and possibly he might make himself useful giving them directions.

"Miss Thompson, are you and Mary going out?" asked David, having been attracted by all the voices in debate at the front door.

"Going to feed ducks, papa," said Mary very seriously, "they will race about and do a lot of quacking."

"I'm sure they will," said David, rocking on his heels and surveying the scene with his hands behind his back. He was conscious he should be doing more in his daughter's company than he had been doing recently. "I hear the guardsmen parade in Green Park too, which is where I suppose you are going."

Claire nodded confirmation of their destination.

"Begging your pardon, my lord," said the butler, "the guards parade there between ten and eleven every morning except Sunday."

"Ah, good, thank you, so you young ladies have missed them for today. In this case, Mary, perhaps you and I could go and see them one morning later this week?"

"Are they riding horses?"

David looked at Ives, the butler, with a raised eyebrow.

"No, Lady Mary," said Ives, "I'm afraid they are foot guards, but even so, they do look very smart in their red uniforms."

Mary frowned. It seemed foot guards were not to her liking, and might even rank lower than ducks.

"In that case, Mary, another day I shall take you to see the Life Guards with their shiny uniforms and on their big black horses in Horse Guards Parade," said David.

"Tomorrow?" she asked, with a hopeful expression on her face.

"I don't know, I might be busy tomorrow, but soon."

Mary's face fell.

He told himself he should determine to make

time for his daughter, not merely do so when he had nothing else to occupy himself and it was thus convenient. After all, she had no family except himself and her grandmother, did she? She had obviously become attached to Miss Thompson, but Miss Thompson might be gone next week. The idea she might be gone so soon, made him feel... unsettled. It was even tempting to go to the park right now, so he could enjoy the walk with both of them.

An annoying little voice of reason said this would be a Bad Idea. Miss Thompson and Mary could walk to the park without anyone who saw them remarking upon it. On the other hand, he was well known and if he was spotted escorting them, it might invite all sorts of questions and speculation he didn't particularly want to answer. Going now was possibly another mistake which could be easily avoided. In the meantime, Mary looked disappointed with him. He realised he had given the wrong answer, both for her and for himself.

"We'll go tomorrow. I shall tell Mr Trevor to find out when they parade at the Horse Guards and he can change any appointments I might have at that time."

Mary clapped her hands enthusiastically, and Claire gave him a smile of warm approval.

They left for the park and he wandered back to his study. Miss Thompson's look of approval had made him feel absurdly pleased with himself for having done something right. He had a suspicion his behaviour had been changing in subtle ways since the arrival of Miss Thompson, although he didn't recall her doing anything to deliberately change him. He wasn't even sure they could be called subtle. However, there was surely something in the household which was different. He recognised his heart lightened when she was around, although he was sure this wasn't it. He didn't think it was all down to the improved behaviour of Mary either, but Miss Thompson was nudging him, consciously or not, about the time he spent with his daughter. Whatever was the cause behind the effect, it was confusing and puzzling, but definitely something to do with Miss Thompson. However, he didn't feel he should pursue this train of thought about an employee any further. It could only lead to problems. But now, before anything else, he needed to send Trevor off to discover when the Horse Guards paraded and then to postpone anything planned for the same time.

In the meantime, Claire and Mary, followed by the footman, had reached the end of the street. Green Park was visible across Piccadilly. Mary tugged at Claire's hand.

"Wait Mary!" said Claire, "this is a very busy road and we must take care not to run in front of a horse or carriage."

Claire knew she hadn't got the skills required of a governess, but at least she could teach her young charge to cross the road safely. Presumably Mary hadn't spent much time where there was traffic.

"We must look both ways to see if it is safe to cross and then down at the road. As we cross, we wouldn't want to step in anything smelly left by the horses, would we?"

Mary giggled. Then Claire made an exaggerated show of looking each way and Mary followed suit. As they did so, an urchin with a broom appeared from nowhere and quickly swept the road for them. As they crossed, the footman tossed a small coin to the boy.

They entered the park through the nearest gate in the park wall and found a large reservoir in front of them. Claire supposed this was what had been described as a pond. Still, never mind, there were ducks on it and nursemaids walking with other small children. Mary ran off towards the water. Claire turned to the footman.

"Can you swim?"

He looked very startled and alarmed.

"No miss. She's not going to fall in is she?"

Claire carefully observed Mary standing near the edge and wondered if she should call to her to take care. At the same time, ducks noticed Mary and, based on their experience, assumed she was about to throw bread to them. Accordingly they swam towards her with some excited quacking. Mary, having limited experience of ducks, stepped back and cast an anxious look at Claire.

"Come over here Mary," said Claire, relaxing, "come and get some bread to throw to them."

A nursemaid, towing a small boy, came in the other direction, heading for the exit. She smiled and nodded to Claire, who instinctively smiled and nodded back. No, doubt, thought Claire, she thinks I am a nursemaid or governess too. Sometimes what you see is what you expect to see. In fact, I not quite sure what I am. I suppose I'm a mixture of not-governess, temporary lady's companion and duck feeder, living in an uncertain limbo.

The footman took a large piece of bread from the bag. Mary reached for it and inexpertly tossed the whole piece towards the flock of ducks. It barely cleared the edge and only just reached the water. The resulting ducky riot made Mary step even further back and uncertainly reach for Claire's hand. Claire took another piece of bread from the footman, moved further along the edge of the pond and crouched down beside Mary.

"Look Mary, let me show you. What we need to do is tear the big piece of bread into little pieces and then throw the little pieces one at a time to the ducks. This way they won't all be arguing over the same big bit of bread."

Claire demonstrated and a few ducks left the big commotion and came to get the smaller offerings. The peaceful result gave Mary confidence to let go of Claire's hand.

"Miss Thompson, may I try?" asked Mary.

Claire gave her a small piece of bread. Mary threw this towards the ducks and the satisfactory behaviour of the ducks had Mary turning back to Claire for more.

Very soon, Mary was disappointed to learn from the footman how all of their bread had been donated to the ducks and there was none left.

"Oh," said Mary, pouting slightly, "some of the ducks might be still be hungry."

"Don't worry," said Claire, "there are more children over there with bread for them too. Look, the ducks are swimming in their direction now."

Mary looked towards the other children with wide eyes and watched what they did. Claire wondered if Mary ever had the chance to play with other children. Emberton Park stood grandly in it's own parkland, and there were no other children to be seen there as far as she knew. Perhaps there were some in the village, but more than likely not of a class who would be allowed to play with Mary. Perhaps here in Mayfair there might be children who would be considered suitable. Claire would have to ask Lord Barton or her ladyship if they knew of any.

"Shall we go home now?" asked Claire, "we could come another day if you like, with some more bread."

"Yes, we'll come back another day," said Mary, "it was fun."

Mary grinned up at Claire who smiled back.

"You will be able to tell your papa, grandmama and Maisie everything about feeding the ducks now," said Claire.

They headed back toward the park exit and Mary skipped along happily in front. Claire recalled how Mary had been described as a 'difficult child, prone to tempers and tantrums'. It seemed to Claire, Mary was a perfectly normal child who had been missing some tender loving care and attention. She hoped they would give Mary their full attention when she chattered to them about ducks, as she undoubtedly would.

As they walked home down Half Moon Street, hand in hand, Claire mused about what other children there might be in the vicinity. She guessed the butler might know, or if he didn't, he could surely find out. She suspected he would have a pretty shrewd idea of everything going on in the street. The servants undoubtedly spoke to the neighbouring servants and probably fraternised during their time off.

"Mary," she said as they entered the house, "run upstairs and tell Maisie about the ducks while I speak to Mr Ives."

Ives turned an enquiring eye in her direction.

"Ives, what other children of Lady Mary's age live nearby? I am conscious she has nobody with whom to play."

"I believe Sir John Wicksteed, has a girl and a boy of a similar age miss. He is a baronet living two doors further down the street and they are in residence at the moment."

"Excellent. I shall speak to her ladyship about them."

"My lord," said Claire at dinner, "Ives tells me a neighbour, Sir John Wicksteed, has two children of similar age to Lady Mary. I wonder if it would be beneficial for the children to be introduced so they may play together?"

"I'm sure it would be," he said, "I remember how enjoyable it was to be playing with my brother when we were young."

Claire was surprised because nobody had spoken of a brother. She wondered why not. Was he a black sheep and not spoken of? Had he died and it was indelicate to mention him? Curiosity get the better of her. Surely nobody would blame her for an innocent question?

"You have a brother?"

"Yes, my younger brother, Roger, is a cavalry captain in Spain with the Marquess of Wellington, which explains why you have not met him."

So much, Claire thought, for lurid suppositions. She had too much imagination.

" Mother, I do not know Sir John. Would it be convenient for you to call on them one morning to make their acquaintance?"

"Yes, Miss Thompson and I could call on them on Thursday to see what they are like. Or, it might need to be Friday or Saturday, depending when the first of Miss Thompson's day dresses are ready."

Barton raised an eyebrow and looked at his mother and then Claire, but passed no comment.

Philippa Carey

Chapter 14 - Wednesday

The next day, at ten thirty, Claire brought Mary downstairs. The earl was waiting for them at the front door, dressed for driving and with a whip in his gloved hands. Through the front door could be seen his curricle with a pair of horses, whose heads were being held by a groom. David looked at Mary with approval as she was looking very smart in a little poke bonnet and had a broad smile on her face. He looked at Miss Thompson and frowned. She was not dressed to go out.

"Miss Thompson, I was expecting you to accompany us, but you have not dressed for the occasion."

"My apologies, my lord, but her ladyship said the modiste was coming this morning for a fitting and I was to remain here."

David was both disappointed and annoyed. He had been looking forward to driving them both down to the Horse Guards parade ground. He told himself it was none of his concern if his mother needed her companion elsewhere. He didn't really convince himself, but there was nothing he could say. Especially not in front of the butler and the footman.

"Papa, never mind," volunteered Mary, "I told you all about the ducks yesterday. So today I said to Miss Thompson I would tell her all about the horses when we get back."

David was slightly taken aback by the assertiveness of his young daughter. However, there seemed to be no reason to disagree.

"Oh. Well. In this case, we must not delay in case we miss some of it, come along."

He offered his hand to Mary and they went down the steps to his curricle. He had thought to use the curricle, as from its elevated position, Mary would be able to see everything which was going on in the parade. He lifted Mary into the seat and she grinned at him, clearly delighted by the whole business. It was a short distance to Horse Guards Road, so they were soon parked on the parade ground. There was a little time to spare before the soldiers arrived and David took the opportunity to explain to Mary what was going to happen. Then, at eleven o'clock precisely, the Life Guards arrived in their bright red and gold uniforms, bobbing atop their large black horses with harnesses jingling.

David reflected how he was finding it rewarding to spend time with his daughter. He had not been doing it all that much recently, largely, he supposed, because Mary had been temperamental and badly behaved. He then realised he had been missing a great deal. It had been all too easy to hand over a fractious girl to one of his servants. Mary had become a different person just recently and it did not escape his notice how the change had happened since the arrival of Miss Thompson. This must be why the idea of her leaving always seemed to him to be depressing.

When they arrived home, it was time for everyone to have lunch. In principle he knew Mary would afterwards be due for a nap, although he wondered if Mary's excitement would have settled enough for her to actually sleep. He would not be surprised if, when she was supposed to be napping, she would instead still be regaling Miss Thompson or her nursery maid of all the details of her outing. In the meantime, while Mary went up to the nursery, he joined his mother and Miss Thompson for a light lunch.

"Barton," said his mother, "Miss Thompson's ball gown was a good fit this morning, so I have sent an acceptance for a ball this evening. Naturally you need to escort us."

He put down his knife and fork, and sat back in astonishment. "Rather sudden isn't it? We've only been here a couple of days. How on earth did they know to send an invitation?"

"I called on Lady Oswald yesterday and it's her granddaughter's coming out ball this evening. Naturally we are invited and I confirmed our attendance a short while ago, as soon as the modiste had left."

Claire was amused by the expression of horror on Barton's face. She already knew about the ball as she had been told straight after her dress fitting. She too, had been surprised to learn about an invitation so soon after their arrival, but she was looking forward to sitting beside the dowager and observing all the dancing.

The dowager turned to Claire. "Lady Oswald and I have been friends since before we were married," she said, by way of added explanation, "so I couldn't miss her granddaughter's debut."

She turned back to her son.

"Don't worry, you won't have to lead the girl out in the opening set, I know you don't much care for her and her father will lead her out anyway. However, I do expect you to do the pretty and ask her for a set soon after, I want her to be a success for my friend's sake."

Barton had a pained expression on his face. Claire looked down at her plate so he wouldn't see her smirking.

Chapter 15

Mary was sitting on a footstool with her rapt attention on Claire. Sally was helping Claire get dressed for the ball. Mary had seen the dress when it was delivered, but not when it was being worn with matching gloves and slippers. Robbins had already been in, briefly, to help Sally arrange Claire's hair and weave in a ribbon to match the dress.

Claire watched in the mirror as Sally arranged the final few tendrils of hair to frame Claire's face. She could see Mary was fascinated by the whole exercise. It brought to mind how Claire herself had watched her mother getting ready for a ball. Claire's heart went out to Mary, who no longer had a mother. It would be a wrench when Mary went off back to the country and Claire went off to who knew where. She hoped the earl would soon find a lady to marry who suited both him and Mary. She also hoped they would find someone suitable as Mary's governess. Claire knew the governess would need to have a gentle and warm personality to win Mary's confidence and affection. However, right now, she had to put these concerns to the back of her mind and make the most of the evening. It might be the only time she would attend a grand ball in the heart of Mayfair.

"All done miss," said Sally standing back.

Claire stood and turned around. "Well done Sally, I can see you are a quick learner. You will make a fine lady's maid very soon."

Sally flushed with pleasure at the praise.

"What do you think Lady Mary?" asked Claire.

"I think you look very beautiful Miss Thompson and all the fine gentlemen will want to dance with you." Mary sighed. "I wish the ball was here in the house so I could see everything."

"You will one day Mary," said Claire, crouching down to her level, "but for now I will tell you all about it tomorrow. In the meantime it's well past your bedtime, so Sally will take you upstairs now to Maisie."

Claire kissed Mary's forehead and received a brief hug in return. As she stood, Claire tried not to think any more about when they would be going their separate ways.

Sally placed a light shawl around Claire's shoulders and then took Mary's hand to lead her up to the nursery.

Claire slowly made her way down the stairs. As she started on the final flight, she could see the earl standing in the hall in his black and white evening dress. She thought he looked extremely handsome and could hardly believe he was to escort her, and his mother, to a ball. She felt as if she was living in a dream. As well as telling Mary about it tomorrow, she would have to write to her sister. Her brothers wouldn't be interested, but her sister would be desperate to hear every last detail of a fashionable ball in Mayfair.

Lord Barton looked up and then she saw him suddenly freeze in blatant admiration. Claire nearly missed a step. The warmth of his regard was unmistakable and it made Claire feel warm too. It was indeed like a dream, but she knew it was for this one evening only. Tomorrow they would be back to normal and in the next week or two they will have gone their separate ways.

The butler had been hovering nearby, holding the earl's hat, while his lordship was putting on his gloves. However, now the earl was standing very still, one glove on and one glove off, his eyes rivetted on Claire. She continued down the stairs, hoping she wouldn't blush at his regard and give her thoughts away. She tried hard to suppress a little satisfied smile at the effect she was having on his lordship.

Motion on the stairs caught David's eye and he glanced up. And stared at the vision on her way down the stairs. He was already aware Miss Thompson was an attractive young lady, but this was.... dramatic. Her ball gown was a sky blue with matching elbow length gloves and an ivory lace overdress. Sky blue slippers peeped out from under her dress as she came downstairs. He wasn't quite sure what they had done with her hair but somehow it emphasised her face in a way which it hadn't before. This was a beautiful young lady in the latest stare of fashion and he couldn't simply see her as his mother's companion any more. Companions didn't look like this.

"Miss Thompson you... ," he said, grasping for words as she reached the bottom of the stairs, "...you look extremely fine this evening."

Fine? Fine? Was that the limit of his eloquence this evening? His attention was then drawn by his mother, now following Miss Thompson down the stairs. She had a small smile on her face and if David wasn't very much mistaken, she looked a little smug. Presumably she was taking credit for Miss Thompson's stunning appearance. It brought his attention back to the here and now, and he put on his second glove before taking his hat from the butler.

It wasn't far to go to the ball, but the carriage was a necessity if they didn't want their slippers and hems to get dirty in the street. Besides, there would be a lot of shocked faces if they arrived on foot like servants. However, since everybody else arrived by carriage, the street was congested and it took ages to travel a mere two streets.

David knew Miss Thompson was from a small village in Kent, after all, he had been franking her letters. However, he hadn't the faintest idea what society might be like in that corner of the county.

"Miss Thompson," said David, who was sitting with his back toward the horses and thus facing the ladies, "have you been to many balls before?"

"Oh no, my lord, well, nothing like this. Sometimes a neighbour would arrange a dinner party and there would be a little dancing afterwards. Then, as well, we used to go to the local monthly assemblies in Maidstone, but I am sure they will bear little comparison to this evening."

"At the local assembly, did you find yourself

dancing with the local butcher and the baker?"

"Oh no. My father would never have permitted us to dance with someone who was not of the gentry or aristocracy." She thought for a moment. "And nobody in trade ever asked us, probably because they knew father would refuse. No doubt they wouldn't want to offend him and lose his custom as well."

The dowager nodded in approval.

"It's not a question which will arise today," said David, "I'm sure there will be no butchers or bakers present."

"And I will not be dancing anyway," added Claire.

"Not dance?" said the dowager in shocked tones, "why ever not?"

"Why not? Because I am your companion, and companions do not dance, do they? It would be unseemly."

"Nonsense! I expect you to dance," said the dowager, "in fact I would not be surprised if your dance card was entirely filled this evening."

Claire was startled into silence.

"I never thought to ask," continued the dowager, "but I suppose from your comments before, you do know how to dance? Cotillions, Quadrilles and country dances, for example?"

"Oh, yes, this is not a problem, I doubt there will be anything I do not know," said Claire, still a little dazed at the prospect.

"What about the waltz?" asked David, "do you know how to waltz?"

"I do know, but I have little experience of it. Waltzing was frowned upon at the local assemblies. I am sure my father would not have approved of it in a public place. No, what little waltzing there was, was at private gatherings, and not at all of those either."

"I have every expectation there will be waltzing this evening. May I stake an early claim to the first one and to the supper dance as well?"

Claire glanced at her ladyship who frowned as she considered the request. "Some people would say you shouldn't waltz until the patronesses of Almack's have given their approval." Then her frown cleared. "But frankly, I don't think we should pay any attention to them. I don't have vouchers for Almack's, nor was I planning to ask for them. So, yes, by all means go ahead and waltz," she said, nodding approval.

Claire felt faintly disappointed, as she would have liked to see Almack's. On the other hand, she was on her way to a large ball in the centre of Mayfair, in a brand new ball gown. Then she was already promised a waltz by a very handsome gentleman. All this was already far more than she had anticipated when she left home, so she could manage quite comfortably without Almack's. Besides, she had heard it was insipid and only considered the place one had to go to, because it was so exclusive and difficult to enter.

"Thank you, my lord, I shall be sure to make a note once I have my dance card."

Claire was looking about her as they joined the receiving line which extended all the way down the stairs. She was trying to be discreet and not gawk at everybody like a country bumpkin. The noise was tremendous, with everybody talking and trying to make themselves heard over all the other people who were also trying to make themselves heard in the entrance way. She didn't know who all these people were, but there were a lot of jewels and elegant dresses in evidence. She felt glad she was wearing a new ball gown, of which the dowager and the earl obviously approved, so she didn't feel out of place or underdressed.

By the time they got to the front of the line at the top of the stairs, they could hear a country dance was already underway. They entered the ballroom with the dowager on one of David's arms and Claire on the other. They paused in the doorway to survey the scene.

"I see Lady Oswald, over on the left, so you may take us there, if you please Barton."

Claire found the ballroom even more overwhelming than the entrance had been. She had attended local assemblies at home, but somehow this was much more intense and the people here looked as if they were trying hard to impress everyone else. At home most people seemed to be more interested in enjoying themselves than showing off in front of people they saw frequently in town. Here there was so much colour, so much noise, so much heat and so many stale odours, not all of which were perfumes. The whole affair was a little intimidating. She was glad to be holding onto the earl's reassuring arm.

"Good evening Anne," said Lady Oswald as they reached her, "who is this you have with you?" She had a small smile on her face, almost as if she already knew the answer.

"This is Miss Thompson, daughter of Baron Hunton, who is my companion for the time being. Miss Thompson, this is my good friend Lady Oswald."

Claire curtseyed to Lady Oswald, who briefly glanced over Claire and then nodded, as if in approval.

"Ladies, good evening," said a young man, who seemed to appear from nowhere and was giving them all a bow. He had a handsome, smiling, boyish face with unfashionable curling sandy hair.

"Barton," he said to the earl with a nod, "I hadn't expected to see you back in town so soon."

Lady Barton and Lady Oswald were already sitting together, ready for a good gossip and apparently paying no attention to the young people.

"It's a long story, which I will tell you later. In the meantime, may I make you known to Miss Thompson, my mother's companion. Miss Thompson, this is Viscount Daintree, a friend of mine from our university days."

He bowed again to Claire who curtseyed back.

"Miss Thompson, may I have the honour of a dance this evening?"

Claire looked towards Lady Barton who glanced up and nodded approval. It seemed she was paying attention after all.

"Not so fast, Daintree, Miss Thompson has

already granted me the honour of a dance, but I have yet to mark her card. I would not wish to have my place stolen."

David took Claire's card and wrote his name in for the first waltz and also for the supper dance, before passing the card to Lord Daintree. He looked at it carefully, before raising a speculative eyebrow at David, who remained impassive. Lord Daintree then put his name down for the country dance which was to follow the one currently in progress, before handing it back to Claire. She saw Barton had chosen the first waltz and the supper dance was yet another waltz. She looked sideways at him, but he was already looking the other way at a lady who had arrived at his side. The lady looked familiar. If Claire was not much mistaken, it was his prospective betrothed, whom Claire had seen at Hemingford Park and then passed rather hurriedly at the entrance.

"Miss Hawksley, good evening," said Barton.

So that was her name, thought Claire. The one I had to keep Mary away from, because Mary was difficult and temperamental. Well, it was her loss, Mary had just craved some attention and kind treatment, in order to change from a difficult child into a lovable one. Hopefully Miss Hawksley will give her that if she becomes Lady Barton. If she doesn't took good care of Mary, I shall be very sorry for Mary and have no sympathy for Miss Hawksley.

"Miss Thompson, our dance I believe," said Lord Daintree, interrupting Claire's thoughts. She hadn't noticed the music had stopped in preparation for the next set. She put her hand on his sleeve and let him lead her to the dance floor.

"Lord Barton, who is the lady whom you brought into the ballroom with her ladyship?" asked Miss Hawksley, as Claire and Lord Daintree walked away.

David thought this was a little nosey and impertinent, but he was determined to remain polite. He would have to ask Miss Hawksley to dance, but it would be only once and it would be a country dance too.

"It is Miss Thompson, her ladyship's new companion. You may recall we borrowed her from Lady Sutton whilst waiting for my daughter's new governess to arrive. Lady Sutton found herself a different companion, so Lady Barton decided to keep Miss Thompson as her own companion whilst we are in London."

"Oh I see. I did not recognise her, but I recall her now from Hemingford Park, when she was dashing through the entrance hall in pursuit of your daughter. I do hope the new governess has arrived, as Miss Thompson was clearly letting the child run wild."

David was getting irritated and feeling defensive of Miss Thompson. He thought Miss Thompson had been doing very well and was a credit to them. She had fitted in so well, it was as if she belonged there. Miss Hawksley clearly had no idea what she was talking about and besides, it was none of her business. It wasn't going to become her business either. Moreover, it would be best if they stopped talking before he said something he might regret. He was sure the current dance was one which didn't permit much conversation.

"May I have this dance, I think they are about to start?"

Miss Hawksley looked smug and put her hand on his sleeve. He hurried her down to the bottom of the set which was nearly complete.

Claire noticed them joining the same set. It wasn't surprising really, if they were to be betrothed before long, but she still found it a little depressing. Lord Daintree caught her eye and he looked concerned. Claire realised she must have been frowning or had looked unhappy. She hoped he didn't think she was reluctant to dance with him. She cleared her mind of Lord Barton and Miss Hawksley and gave Daintree what she hoped was a friendly and reassuring smile. It would never do if other gentlemen thought she was morose and an unwilling dancer. This was could be her only chance to dance at a grand London ball. She needed to make the most of it and hope other gentlemen would ask her to dance.

She need not have worried. Every time her partner returned her to Lady Barton, more gentlemen appeared, asking for an introduction. Very soon her card was full for the rest of the evening. She didn't know what the older ladies were talking about, but Lady Barton was looking very pleased with herself and Lady Oswald seemed to be still regarding Claire with approval. Claire relaxed, as it appeared her dancing was as good and as elegant as the older ladies could wish. She had been a little worried her dancing might have looked provincial, or even slightly rustic, although she had always thought herself competent.

Before long she heard the opening strains of a waltz and Lord Barton appeared at her elbow.

"Miss Thompson, our dance I believe?" he said with a slight bow.

She said nothing, but gave him a shy smile and took his hand to be guided onto the dance floor. For a moment it crossed her mind to wonder why he was waltzing with her, instead of Miss Hawksley. Had he not realised Miss Hawksley would be here at the ball, before he had marked Claire's card? The very next moment, she knew she didn't care how it was or had come about. Right here, right now, he was her partner and she was going to be in his arms until the music ended. She finally confessed to herself it was what she had wanted for some time, but hadn't dared to recognise. She, or he, might be gone in a matter of days, so now was the time to create a memory which would sustain her in the possibly bleak years ahead.

She put her left hand onto his shoulder and somehow, she didn't know how, her right hand found his left. She looked into his eyes as he swept her into the dance. As they moved around the dance floor there was only him and her. They said nothing. Everything else, and everyone else, faded into a background blur, with only the sound of the music marking their movement around the ballroom. All too soon the music ended, the world intruded upon them again and they came to a halt. Claire took a deep breath and stepped back ever so slightly, but they kept looking at each other, as they stood motionless for a long moment.

David looked around, then put her hand back on his sleeve.

"Thank you for the dance, Miss Thompson, allow me to return you to Lady Barton," he said.

Claire was sure he sounded slightly breathless. Had he found the dance energetic or had he been as affected by her as she had been of him?

Claire gradually regained her composure over the following country dances. Later she realised she couldn't remember who her partners had been and hoped she hadn't seemed too vague and absent minded. She made a mental note to hang onto her dance card as a reminder. At least if she knew the names, she could pretend to remember them if she met them again. Before long, it was time for the supper dance which meant she was going to be waltzing once more with Lord Barton. This time she knew what effect he was going have upon her, so she would, she hoped, be less disconcerted. Perhaps if she wasn't quite so dazed, she would be able to savour the dance more.

In the event, it didn't help a great deal. This time, as she was held in his arms, she was also held spellbound once more. At the end of the waltz, she once more found herself blinking as the rest of the world came back into focus.

"Thank you again, Miss Thompson," said David, "my only regret is how propriety forbids me from asking you for a third dance."

Claire stared at him wide-eyed in surprise. He

wanted to dance with her again? What about Miss Hawksley? Was Miss Hawksley's dance card too full? Wait, was he flirting with her? With his mother's companion?

"With me?" squeaked Claire, feeling foolishly inarticulate.

"Yes, Miss Thompson, with you. In the meantime, I'm afraid we must join my mother and so I may lead both of you into supper."

Claire tucked her hand into his elbow as he led her across the room to where his mother and Lady Oswald were seated.

"Ladies, may I lead you in to supper?"

The ladies remained sitting in their chairs.

"No, no, Barton, you go ahead with Miss Thompson," said his mother, "Lady Oswald and I have much to talk about. We are happy to lead each other into supper, when we are good and ready, are we not Dorothy?"

"Oh certainly, you young people run along," said Lady Oswald, trying and failing to suppress a grin, "off you go, we don't need you." She flicked her fingers at them in a gesture of dismissal.

David hesitated a moment, clearly caught by surprise.

Claire's eyes flicked from one lady to the other as well. She had not expected this either. Not that she minded. In fact she was secretly more than happy to dine alone with Lord Barton. Even if 'alone' was in a room filled with other people.

Lord Barton took her into the supper room and made a beeline for a small table in the corner which only had two chairs against it.

"Please take a seat, Miss Thompson, and I shall fill a couple of plates for us."

Before he went off, he took a couple of glasses of champagne from a passing waiter and placed them on the table. Claire took a cautious sip. She was used to wine, but had been warned the bubbles in champagne were liable to make her tipsy, especially on an empty stomach. The very last thing she needed at this point was to lose her head. And not in any other sense either.

Claire gazed, without seeing, into the middle distance. She contemplated how she was failing as a companion by not staying with Lady Barton, and instead, almost running off to dine with her son. It seemed wrong somehow, and not likely to encourage her ladyship to keep Claire as a companion for much longer, although this had always been an unlikely prospect.

It had been Claire's decision to leave her family and become a companion to an older lady. At the time it had felt like a way to take control of her own life. Now it was starting to feel as if she had lost all control and was being swept along by events over which she really had no control at all. On the one hand, at present she had a comfortable and fairly luxurious position. On the other hand, she had no idea where she would be, or what she would be doing, a mere month from now. She was trying not to think about it too much, but the uncertainty was uncomfortable.

Her focus returned to the immediate as Lord Barton put two plates on the table.

"I hope my choices meet with your approval as I

realised I had no idea of your preferences," he said.

Claire wasn't sure if she would even notice what she was eating when it was Lord Barton sitting facing her. She felt obliged to glance at the plate.

"It all looks delicious, my lord."

"Barton, please, not my lord. Or, if you wish, in private, David."

Claire took in a sharp breath. This was surely getting too personal. She needed common sense and to keep her distance, for everybody's comfort.

"If you please sir, I shall limit myself to Barton in private if you don't mind, anything else would not be proper. I am after all, your mother's employee."

"Technically you may be correct, but I find myself thinking of you more as a guest of my mother, rather than her employee."

Claire looked up from her plate and over Barton's shoulder saw Miss Hawksley glaring at her from another table. She shifted slightly in her seat so Miss Hawksley was not visible beyond Lord Barton. However, it did make her wonder why the other young lady was not sitting in her place opposite his lordship.

"Please excuse my asking... Barton, would it not be more appropriate for you to be dining with Miss Hawksley rather than me?"

"Miss Hawksley? Absolutely not. She is no more than an acquaintance and will remain, at best, a distant one if she makes any more remarks about yourself or Lady Mary."

"Remarks?"

"Nothing of importance or which have any value in being repeated. Forget Miss Hawksley and tell me something of your family."

Claire blinked in surprise. Was Miss Hawksley not in line to be the next Countess Barton? Had she misunderstood the situation completely? No, surely not? She had seen them riding away and looking cosy together in his curricle. By the sound if it, Miss Hawksley had made some careless remarks. Nobody paid much attention to comments about the servants, like her, but if she had said something disparaging about Lady Mary, no wonder Barton was annoyed. Lady Mary wasn't even six years old yet, so it wasn't reasonable to expect her to be an angel all the time. Despite the warnings about Mary being spoilt and difficult, Claire thought Mary behaved well once she had some sympathetic care and undivided attention. Was Claire being used to put Miss Hawksley in her place? No doubt, once the earl's annoyance had subsided, the beautiful Miss Hawksley would be forgiven, especially if Claire was no longer there to be remarked upon.

Claire stopped woolgathering and focussed on Barton. He was sitting there with a raised eyebrow, obviously waiting for an answer to his question. What was it? Oh yes.

"My parents live in the village of Farleigh Green in Kent, not very far from Maidstone and the Dover Road. I suppose you know this already from franking my letters?"

He nodded.

"Is it a large house?" he asked.

"Compared to Hemingford Park, no, it is tiny. However in a small village like Farleigh Green, it is the largest house. It all depends on what is being compared, does it not? Anyway, there are two tenant farms, which are equally small and not very profitable. So we are not a wealthy family and society is very limited too. It got to the point where I felt suffocated and had to get away. Becoming a companion to an elderly lady was my only realistic choice."

"You have no family you could have gone to?"

"I only have Uncle Alan and Aunt Marjorie who live in a village called Cley on the north Norfolk coast. Frankly I doubt they would have known what to do with me, as I don't suppose there is much society there either. We don't have much contact with them. A letter every Christmas is about all."

Claire wondered briefly why she was telling him all these things. Perhaps it was because he was the first person she could have a proper conversation with since she left home. Mary was too young, the dowager didn't encourage it and the servants were at arm's length.

"I notice you do write frequently to your family."

"I write to my parents to reassure them I am safe and well. They had grave doubts of the wisdom of my leaving home. I write to my sister because I know she is desperate to know everything. I shall have to write her a long letter tomorrow describing the ball, but fear not, I shall mention no names."

"She is a younger sister?"

"Yes, she is just sixteen. I also have two brothers of thirteen and eleven, but I'm sure they have no interest in a letter from their sister, because then they would be obliged to reply."

"Are the boys at school?"

"Yes, but just the local school. Father went to Harrow and then Cambridge, but both are out of reach for my brothers."

"So did you leave home to lighten your father's financial burden?"

Claire hesitated, but realised Barton had already worked out money was tight in the Thompson family. Why else would she be a paid companion? Perhaps she should have said less, but it really didn't matter now.

"That was my excuse, but in reality I just needed to get away. I don't suppose the village of Wicken would have been much of an improvement on Farleigh Green, but it would have been different and the faces would have been different too."

"I am sure it has all been different, just not the different you expected," said David.

Claire gave a wry smile and then looked down at her empty plate. When had she eaten it all?

"I think, Miss Thompson, we should make our way back into the ballroom as the supper room is emptying."

Claire picked up her glass to finish her champagne, but it was mysteriously empty too.

"May I suggest a third glass would be inadvisable?" said the earl with a smile, "assuming you plan to dance some more. It would not do to be unsteady on your feet."

Claire was horrified. Two glasses and she hadn't even noticed it being refilled? Was this why her tongue was so loose? And he had noticed? She might need to tell her next partner, whoever it was, she was too hot to dance and would prefer to promenade instead.

Chapter 16 - Thursday

Claire arose late the next morning and took a light breakfast in her room. As soon as she was dressed, she went upstairs to the nursery. Lady Mary had been promised an account of the ball.

"Miss Thompson, you're awake!" said Mary, dropping her toys as soon as she saw Claire in the doorway. Mary ran across the room and flung her arms around Claire's legs, before looking up.

"Did you see all the flowers?" asked Mary.

"Flowers?"

"All the flowers downstairs. The footman said they were all for you."

"I don't know anything about flowers for me."

"Come and see," Mary grabbed Claire's hand and dragged her out of the nursery, down the stairs and into the morning room.

They stopped just inside the doorway.

"There! See? Lots and lots of flowers, all for you."

An astounded Claire walked to the nearest vase, which was full of roses, and took out the card. Baron Rogers? Claire couldn't remember exactly who he was, but concluded he must have been one of her dance partners from last night. Thank goodness she had had the foresight to hang onto her dance card. She went around the other bouquets, reading the cards, in a daze. She had danced every set, but never expected this deluge of blooms. Why would all the gentlemen be sending them to a penniless nobody like her? Surely they didn't all intend courting her?

"You made quite an impact less night," said a

male voice from the doorway. "I would have sent you flowers myself, except it would have seemed a bit odd to be sending them to my own house."

Claire whirled to face Lord Barton.

"But.... but... I don't understand. Why would these gentlemen send flowers to me? I'm just her ladyship's companion. It doesn't seem right or proper somehow."

"Ah, but Miss Thompson, you underestimate yourself. They didn't see you as just a companion, they saw you as a beautiful young woman who danced divinely."

Claire felt herself blushing and a small hand creep into hers.

"Papa, did you dance with Miss Thompson?"

"Yes, I did. Twice. I would have liked to have danced with her more than twice, but it would have started a lot of talk."

"Talk? What sort of talk?" asked Mary.

"Mary, it's time we went back upstairs," said Claire, who was now blushing furiously. She drew Mary back towards the door. David, who had a broad smile on his face, stepped aside.

As they went back upstairs, Mary asked again.

"Miss Thompson, what did my papa mean by talk?"

Claire saw Mary was going to be persistent and an answer was going to be necessary, before they could move on to some other topic.

"Gentlemen don't dance more than twice with a lady unless they are married or engaged to be married. If he danced a third time with me, people would think we are betrothed. Of course, we are not and are not going to be, so it would have been very embarrassing for both of us."

Mary was quiet for a long time, almost until they reached the nursery.

"Wouldn't you like to marry my papa? I think it would be a very good idea."

"Mary! Enough. Let us talk about something else if you please."

It was a question which Claire didn't want to answer. She didn't want to lie to Mary and she knew, yes, she would like to marry Lord Barton. She admitted to herself she loved him. But it couldn't happen. After all, she was a servant. Granted she was an upper servant, but still a servant and she had nothing she could bring to such a marriage. After all, if her father could afford a dowry, she wouldn't be working as a companion in the first place.

Before long, Sally appeared in the nursery.

"Please miss, her ladyship said she intends to call on Lady Wicksteed this morning. She says you are to wear one of the new day dresses and be ready in half an hour."

The dowager, accompanied by Claire, who was suitably arrayed a new dress, called at the Wicksteed's house. She gave the butler one of her cards and he disappeared upstairs, returning only moments later. For Mary's sake, Claire hoped the Wicksteeds would be amiable and their children friendly.

"Lady Wicksteed is at home my lady and begs you will follow me to the morning room."

They traipsed upstairs to where he opened a door and announced "The Dowager Countess Barton, milady"

"Lady Barton how nice to meet you," said a young Lady Wicksteed, "and how good of you to call."

"May I introduce my companion, Miss Thompson," said the dowager, and Lady Wicksteed sniffed and nodded to Claire rather dismissively.

Claire was not impressed. Lady Wicksteed was assuming Claire was of no consequence. It was true Claire had little consequence in society, but it was a rash assumption to make when she was companion to the dowager countess of a large and important earldom. Perhaps Lady Wicksteed had no clear idea of who Lady Barton actually was. In any case, Lady Wicksteed's attitude was hardly polite. If she only knew, Lady Wicksteed had no reason to look down her nose at Claire, whose father outranked her husband. Lady Barton had a clear idea of her position in society, but had never behaved like this to Claire or even to the servants. Lady Wicksteed should be grateful Lady Barton had decided to honour her with a visit. Claire clenched her teeth, determined not to let her irritation show. She was here, after all, for Lady Mary's, not Claire's, benefit.

They took seats as a maid arrived with a tea tray.

"I understand you have two children," said Lady Barton, getting to the point without delay.

"Yes, indeed, I have Thomas who is six and Alice who is four, nearly five."

"I have a granddaughter, Lady Mary, aged almost six, who has no companion of her own age. Miss

Thompson learnt of your children, and wondered if they might be suitable playmates for each other."

"I'm sure we can consider it, I shall speak to Sir John when he returns from the House of Commons."

The conversation continued along trivial lines for another fifteen minutes before the dowager declared it was time for them to go.

As they walked back to their own house, Claire couldn't resist any longer.

"I'm sorry, but I did not like her attitude."

"Nor I. She has an excessively high opinion of herself and is quite graceless. I suppose she married into the title and her mother couldn't tell her how to go on."

Claire did wonder if it was the opposite. It could be she had married down. For all Claire knew, Lady Wicksteed was the daughter of a duke and marrying a baronet had been a love match. Whether she was or not, she could be more graceful. Claire hoped she would soon realise the extent of her mistake and social gaffe and bitterly regret it. No, Claire did not like her.

The dowager was shaking her head slowly.

"If it wasn't for Mary," she continued, "I would have nothing further to do with them. I can't imagine you behaving like it once you are married and mistress of your own house."

Claire turned a startled face towards Lady Barton. What was she imagining? Surely she wasn't making assumptions based on the events of a single ball? Were the number of bouquets Claire had received this morning giving Lady Barton wild ideas?

Later that day, Lady Barton was at home to visitors. She made it very clear to Claire she expected her companion to sit with her, as in addition to visitors to her ladyship, there would certainly be gentlemen visitors calling on Claire. Claire was a bit discomfitted by the idea, as the expected attention could come to little, but at the same time she couldn't help feeling a bit flattered at the prospect of gentleman calling on her. If she wasn't mistaken, her ladyship looked rather smug about the whole business. Claire supposed she ought to have expected a number of gentlemen to be calling on her, after seeing the many bouquets which had been delivered in the morning, but even so, it was not a situation familiar to her. As well, it was all very good, to be having these callers, but none of them had stirred her emotions at the ball as did Barton. And in any case, it was all futile. After she left Lady Barton and took up a new post with some other lady, would these gentlemen even know where she had gone? Not only this, but the change of post would remind them all she was a lady's companion, a servant, not a baron's daughter worthy of courting any more. Claire realised she might even be presumptuous thinking they were coming to court her. They might be just going through the motions, as would expected by convention. She supposed she should enjoy the attention while it lasted.

The earl joined them just as his friend Lord Daintree was announced.

"Lady Barton, Miss Thompson, good afternoon," said Daintree, bowing.

"Good afternoon, Lord Daintree," she said. At least, this gentleman was one she remembered from last night, perhaps because it was the first one she had been introduced to at the ball. While she had been upstairs, she had taken the opportunity to collect her dance card and look through it again, trying to remember who all the gentlemen were. She had slipped it into the pocket of her dress, just in case she needed to take a surreptitious look at it.

"Miss Thompson I am hoping you might allow me to drive you in the park tomorrow afternoon?"

A drive in the park? Was Lord Daintree serious in his attentions? Claire could see no future in it but driving in the park would be nice. Something to remember and something more to tell her sister too. She looked at Lady Barton, whose approval she would need, before accepting the invitation. The dowager nodded agreement. Claire supposed Daintree was well known to her ladyship if Daintree and Barton were old friends. She noticed Barton was a bit stony-faced. Did he know something about his friend which his mother did not? Never mind, she couldn't come to much harm in Hyde Park could she?

"Thank you, my lord, it will be most enjoyable," she said.

"Shall we say four o'clock?"

"Yes, my lord, four o'clock will be most convenient."

Claire was intrigued. She knew of the parade at four o'clock called the Fashionable Hour and would happy to see it, if only once. Claire would have agreed to almost any time, but she knew this would mean she would see, and be seen, by much of society as they promenaded in the park.

Chapter 17 - Friday

Lady Barton had received a note from the Wicksteeds to say they would call on Saturday afternoon with their children. The dowager and Claire were not over-enthused at the prospect, but it was for Mary's benefit, so they resolved to receive them and therefore returned a note to say it would be convenient in the late afternoon. Claire was glad they were coming on Saturday, not today, as she wanted to be there when the children met. Since Lord Wicksteed was coming too, she wondered if they had now discovered exactly who the Bartons were and consequently were keen to make amends for Lady Wicksteed's previous off-hand manner.

Later on, Claire was hovering on the landing within earshot of the front door just before four o'clock. Claire knew it was unfashionable to appear eager, but regardless, she really was eager to have a drive in the park with a smart gentleman beside her. The opportunity was not likely to come her way again.

The knocker sounded and the butler stepped forward to open the door. Claire peeped over the banister to see if it was Lord Daintree as expected. It was. As he was speaking to the butler, obviously asking for her, she started down the stairs. The movement caught his eye, he stopped speaking to the butler and, with a smile, watched her come downstairs.

"Good afternoon Miss Thompson, I'm glad to see

133

you are ready, so my horses won't be kept standing for long."

She didn't have a chance to reply before a small female voice behind her spoke up.

"Lord Daintree, have you brought your curricle and a pair?"

Daintree leant sideways and looked around Claire to see Lady Mary following her. Claire turned to see her as well and noticed Mary was dressed to go out. She then also noticed Lord Barton was following his daughter down the stairs.

"Yes, Lady Mary I have. I am about to take Miss Thompson for a drive in the park."

"My papa took me in his curricle to see the changing of the Horse Guards. It was very good but Miss Thompson couldn't come because she had to visit the modiste."

Claire opened her mouth to stem the flow of unnecessary information, but hesitated as she caught Barton's eye. He merely shook his head slightly as if he didn't mind Mary's chatter to his friend.

"Miss Thompson," continued Mary, "can I come with you in the curricle today?"

"Mary, hush, I don't think Lord Daintree will want two of us in his carriage," said Claire.

"Lord Daintree, do you mind if I come too? My papa says your horses are some of the best and I would really like to see how they go."

Daintree was flummoxed by the idea of a small girl being a judge of horseflesh. He looked mutely at Barton who said nothing, but Claire thought the earl looked faintly amused. Daintree then looked back at

Claire who was speechless and entirely baffled by the whole situation.

"Lady Mary I would be happy to take you in my curricle some time..." said Daintree.

Unfortunately, Mary interpreted right now as 'some time' after having been taken by her father to the Horse Guards in his curricle.

"Thank you, thank you," said Mary, clapping her hands, "come along Miss Thompson, let's go!"

She grabbed Claire's hand, dragging her toward the open doorway. Claire glanced back at the two men, wondering why they didn't do or say something. Daintree was glaring with narrowed eyes at Barton. Barton was smirking back at his friend. As Mary hurried her down the steps, Claire saw how Barton had contrived to send a five year old chaperone with her and Lord Daintree. She hoped he was just playing a trick on his friend, although Barton hadn't looked very pleased when the invitation had been made. Lady Barton appeared to approve of Daintree, so... Could it be Barton was jealous of his friend and wished he had invited her first? Claire's heart lightened as she helped Mary up into the carriage. If he was jealous, it could only mean he had feelings for her. When he had said he would have wanted to dance with her a third time, perhaps he wasn't just joking or flirting. Could he have meant it?

Philippa Carey

Chapter 18 - Saturday

After breakfast on Saturday, Claire had presented herself in the earl's study.

"Good morning, Miss Thompson, please take a seat," he said, "this morning I am expecting some candidates for the post of governess to Lady Mary. I would like you to sit in on them and then afterwards give me your opinion as to which one you think will suit Mary best."

Ah, thought Claire, more than likely it wasn't going to be long before they all went back to Hemingford Park. Never mind, it had been good while it lasted.

"Very good sir, but might I suggest Lady Mary sit with us as well?"

"Lady Mary? Do you think it appropriate? Why do you suggest it?"

"Well sir, she has taken against governesses in general as her experience with the last one was... less than harmonious."

"Less than harmonious?"

"Lady Mary is strong willed and in addition it appears her last governess had little patience and a quick temper. I gather every time Mary found something difficult, she was punished so as to motivate her to do better. It seems it drove Mary to rebellion rather than motivation, and the governess to despair, hence her abrupt departure."

He looked pensive and shook his head slightly.

"Now I understand," he said, "I see also I have been remiss. I had not fully understood before exactly what had happened with the governess."

"Therefore sir, I suggest Lady Mary sit with us. However, we should perhaps describe the candidates as teachers, not governesses. Then, if she expresses a positive opinion about one of the candidates it might get everything started on the right foot."

"And if she is negative about them all?"

"Then I think it might be wise to ask for more candidates. In the meantime I shall explain to Mary what we are doing and how they are teachers, not governesses, to try and get her in a receptive frame of mind."

Claire was subjected to a thoughtful scrutiny as he considered her words. She hoped he would agree. Mary was a happy girl these days and Claire didn't want to see her distressed by another unfeeling governess.

"Very well. Please do your best with Mary and the two of you will be called when they arrive. We shall use my late wife's sitting room. It is large enough without making the situation too grand or formal. It is not in use these days, as my mother prefers her own sitting room or else the morning room if she has visitors."

Claire stood, curtsied and headed for the nursery floor.

About an hour later Claire went with Mary down to the late countess's sitting room where they sat together on a small sofa. Claire looked around with interest. It was clearly a feminine room, yet was devoid of any small personal items or magazines, which somehow made it feel abandoned. Facing them were two chairs with arms, either side of a small table upon which there was a small bell. The earl came in and sat in one of those chairs.

"Mary," he said, "did Miss Thompson explain what we are going to do?"

Mary nodded, but Claire noticed she looked a little worried. Claire put her arm around Mary's shoulders and Mary inched a little closer. Barton studied them for a brief moment, before the door opened and he looked that way.

"Miss Bradford, my lord," said the butler. Miss Bradford came in, the butler withdrew, the earl stood and Miss Bradford curtsied. Miss Bradford was tall, thin, probably in her fifties and her face was as plain as her dress.

"Good morning Miss Bradford, please take a seat." He gestured towards the sofa. "This is Miss Thompson, my mother's companion and my daughter Lady Mary."

Miss Bradford looked at the sofa with a raised eyebrow before turning back to the earl. Claire supposed she was wondering at the presence of herself and Mary, when she was expecting to be interviewed by the earl alone.

"Please tell us a little about yourself Miss Bradford," said Lord Barton.

Miss Bradford recounted where she had been employed by a titled family until her charges, two girls, no longer needed a governess.

Mary turned sharply and looked up at Claire with an angry frown. Claire put her finger to her lips to say to Mary to stay quiet. Mary crossed her arms and look mutinous, but said nothing.

139

Once Miss Bradford had left the room, Claire turned to Mary.

"Well what do you think?"

Mary scowled at Claire.

"She's a governess," she said crossly, "you said they would be teachers, not governesses."

"She used to be a governess, but she can be just a teacher now."

"Well I don't like her."

Claire looked at David with a sigh. He shrugged and rang the bell. Moments later the butler opened the door again and intoned, "Miss Fairfax, my lord."

Miss Fairfax was a pleasant motherly looking figure, perhaps in her early forties.

Once again David introduced everyone and invited her to talk about herself. After a brief mention of where she had been employed, she looked at Mary

"Lady Mary, what do you like to do best of all?"

Mary looked a little startled at a question suddenly directed at her, but she recovered quickly.

"I like to ride Moonbeam," she said.

"You like to ride moonbeams?" said Miss Fairfax, with a puzzled glance at Claire for clarification.

"Moonbeam is Lady Mary's pony," explained Claire, "she is fast becoming a very good rider."

Miss Fairfax's face cleared with understanding and Mary looked delighted with the praise.

"Oh I see. That's nice, I used to have a pony when I was little."

"What was your pony called?" asked Mary.

"She was called Diamond because she had a diamond shaped white patch on her head." Miss

Fairfax traced the outline of a diamond shape on her own forehead.

Mary had big eyes and mouthed a silent 'oh' as she considered it.

"Do you still ride Miss Fairfax?" asked the earl.

"Not for many years, sir, there is little opportunity for someone in my position, especially here in town."

"If I gave you the position, there could be the opportunity to ride one of our mares alongside Lady Mary."

"I should like that sir."

Claire saw the earl nod with approval. She felt a stab of jealousy. Miss Fairfax was not much older than the earl, very presentable and already knew how to ride. Clearly Lord Barton envisaged riding about the Buckinghamshire estate in the company of his daughter and her attractive governess.
Meanwhile Claire would be fetching and carrying for the dowager until such time as she was no longer needed.

Miss Fairfax turned back to Mary.

"What else do you like to do? Do you like reading and writing?"

"I like reading, but I need help with the long words."

Mary glanced up at Claire, who nodded sympathetically.

"And writing is very difficult. Would you smack my fingers if I made a mistake?"

"No, certainly not. We all make mistakes at the beginning. As your reading gets better, I'm sure your writing will get better too. Besides, there are other things to try as well, like drawing, sewing and singing."

"Miss Fairfax, do you play an instrument?" asked David.

"I play the pianoforte but somewhat indifferently, I'm afraid. It would be enough to get a beginner started, but after a while it would be advisable to engage a music tutor."

The conversation continued like this for a while before Miss Fairfax was asked to step outside.

"Well, what do you think?" asked David.

"I like her," said Mary.

Claire was not surprised. Anybody who liked horses was likely to gain Mary's approval. However, Claire had to admit, although somewhat grudgingly, that Miss Fairfax would probably be a good choice, so she nodded her agreement.

David rang the bell again and the butler ushered in the next candidate.

"Mrs Pomfrey, my lord," he said before retreating and drawing the door closed as he left.

Mrs Pomfrey was a very large lady with grey hair and a forbidding aspect. She told the earl, in rather unemotional tones, how she had been in charge of two boys until they went away to school.

As she was doing so, Claire thought how if she was a six year old girl, she might find Mrs Pomfrey rather intimidating and overwhelming. She glanced down at Mary, who looked a little worried, and surmised Mary thought the same. Claire thought her two young brothers would hesitate to cross Mrs

142

Pomfrey too. No, she couldn't see Mrs Pomfrey as a good choice. Miss Fairfax was the obvious winner. It was depressing in a way. If Claire had had the necessary skills, she would have loved to have the position. She had grown very fond of Mary and had developed a certain affection for Mary's grandmother too. And, Claire felt foolish to admit to herself, she felt affection for Mary's father too. More than simple affection, and this would be unwise, because there could be no future there. No, even if she had the skills, becoming Lady Mary's governess would be a bad idea. Most likely, Miss Fairfax would take over the care of Mary very soon and then Claire would occupy herself with the dowager alone. Even this would probably not last very long and would end just as soon her ladyship returned to Hemingford Park.

Mrs Pomfrey departed and his lordship looked towards Claire and Mary.

"I am supposing the second one, Miss Fairfax, is the one you favour?" he said.

"Yes, papa, she was nice, I liked her. Will she be my teacher?"

He looked at Claire who nodded agreement.

"It seems we agree, so I shall speak to her again. In the meantime, I suggest you two go upstairs for an early luncheon and to get changed. Remember we are going to Astley's Amphitheatre to see the horses and the clowns straight afterwards."

Mary jumped to her feet and pulled Claire towards the door.

"Come along Miss Thompson, we have to hurry

and get ready," she said.

Claire and David exchanged amused smiles at Mary's eagerness, as if Mary thought it would make everything happen sooner. They had not mentioned the Wicksteeds, there was time to tell Mary about them after returning from Astley's.

David knew Mary had been keen to come to Astley's, but he hadn't expected it to be such a great success for them. His daughter was enthralled. She was gazing with big eyes at the performers as they performed their tricks, then the next moment she was jumping up and down, clapping her hands.

"Papa, papa, did you see that?" she would say, clutching his sleeve, then she would turn to Miss Thompson.

"Miss Thompson, that was very clever, wasn't?"

Miss Thompson was obviously enjoying herself too, but David was sure a lot of her pleasure was in Mary's reaction to the show. David knew he had a broad smile on his own face too. He was delighted to see Mary enjoying herself so very much. It had been a brilliant idea to bring his horse-mad daughter here. Of course, it had been Miss Thompson's suggestion, although by all accounts, she had never come here herself until now. He looked over Mary's head at her. She was definitely enjoying the show enormously as well, although without the same physical exuberance as Mary. It had probably been a wise decision of his mother not to come. She wasn't given to emotional displays and she might have been embarrassed by the wild excitement of her granddaughter. As he looked at Miss Thompson, she looked up from Mary and their eyes locked as they smiled at each other. After a moment, she went a little pink in the face and suddenly looked back towards the performers.

She was a very attractive young lady, he thought, and her new walking dress of sage green in the latest style gave her a very elegant air. Nobody looking at her would suppose she was a servant. In a sense she wasn't, as a companion wasn't properly a servant was she? Admiring the appearance of a female servant was unwise and improper. Admiring a well-born companion to his mother was surely acceptable?

He glanced around at the audience. It was a mixture of various walks of life. Many people appeared to be middle class families and others, such as themselves, appeared to be gentry or aristocratic families. He felt a moment of surprise. No doubt the three of them, himself, his daughter and Miss Thompson, did look like a family as well to anybody who didn't know them. It was a new idea which he hadn't considered before. He looked again at Miss Thompson, this time more thoughtfully.

As they reached home in Half Moon Street, Mary was still chattering away nineteen to the dozen about all the things she had seen. A footman lowered the carriage steps and David went down first. He turned and handed Mary down. As he did so, she announced she had to tell grandmama all about the show, and went racing up the steps and into the house. Claire opened her mouth to tell her to slow down, but she was too late, Mary was already gone.

She closed her mouth and looked at David in dismay. He just grinned and shrugged, before offering Claire his hand. As she stepped down onto the flagstones, he found he was curiously reluctant to let go of her hand. She looked a little startled. He promptly let go. He was not going to start talk amongst the servants who were standing around. Of course, if he had been handing down his wife, nobody would have remarked upon it, would they? It was an interesting idea, he thought, as he followed her into the house. Now she wasn't properly a servant, there was nothing wrong with him being attracted to her, was there? Mind you, it might be entirely one-sided if her reaction, when he had handed her down from the carriage, was anything to go by. He wondered if he could take her for a drive in the park tomorrow? No, he thought, tomorrow was Sunday and his mother would not approve. They would be going to church tomorrow and then remaining at home. A drive in the park would have to wait until Monday. However, he could issue the invitation before anyone else thought of it. Like Daintree again, for example.

Chapter 19

After changing her clothing, Claire went to the drawing room to find Mary still chattering to her grandmother as they sat on a sofa. A grandmother who was looking more serious than Claire would have expected. Mary's nursemaid was there too, but looking amused and trying not to show it. Barton followed Claire into the room. The dowager looked up.

"Mary," said her grandmother, "I need to speak to your father and Miss Thompson, you can tell me the rest later. Go upstairs now with Maisie, it must be nearly time for your tea."

She waited for them to depart.

"Barton, close the door and then the two of you sit over here."

Claire wondered what this was all about. Clearly her ladyship was angry about something, but Claire couldn't imagine what it was. Could Mary have said something which was misunderstood by Mary or her grandmother?

"I had a visit this morning from Lady Oswald," said the dowager, "she tells me Lord Daintree, Lady Mary, and you Miss Thompson, were seen driving together in Hyde Park yesterday. Is this true?"

Claire nodded. "Yes, milady."

"Did you know about this Barton?"

"Yes, I was at the door when they left."

The dowager looked at one, then the other, her lips pressed together. There was a long pause.

"Did neither of you consider how this might have appeared?" she said, and thumped the arm of the sofa with her hand.

Claire and the earl looked at each other, both frowning in incomprehension.

"For goodness sake," said an exasperated dowager, "are you both as stupid as each other? Daintree has been seen promenading in the park with an unknown young lady and her daughter! Very soon it will be gossip throughout the ton how my companion is really Daintree's mistress and she has a natural daughter by him!"

Claire's eyes grew wide and her mouth dropped open as she realised what her ladyship meant. And what people would say. It was a disaster. She saw she would inevitably be sent home at once and nobody would employ her as a companion now. Not in London anyway, or anywhere else she might be recognised. Could she even find a post very far away like in the north of England or Scotland? No. It was over. She would spend the rest of her life in Farleigh Green. She sagged in her chair with closed eyes. She was ruined as far as the ton was concerned and all for the sake of a drive in the park.

"No, surely not," said the earl, "everybody knows Daintree is my friend, as soon as they put two and two together, they will realise it is not the case."

His mother said nothing but just stared at him for several minutes with gimlet eyes.

"We should be grateful to Lady Oswald for coming to see me this morning," she said at length, "fortunately, she knew the truth of the matter.

However, once gossip starts, it does not matter whether or not it is true or false. If enough people say it, it becomes true. As it is, the intended visit by the Wicksteeds this afternoon was suddenly cancelled."

She shook her head and sighed.

"They have met Miss Thompson and know Lady Mary is my granddaughter. They must be supposing the girl in the curricle was someone else, since they haven't met Lady Mary. Well, they are fools and certainly not going to meet her now."

Barton sighed and dropped his head, shaking it slightly.

"I'm sorry mother, I'm sorry Miss Thompson, it's all my fault. I was intending to ask Miss Thompson to drive out with me, but Daintree asked first. I was irritated with him and put the idea into Mary's head to go with them. I never thought of the possible consequences. I'm sorry for Mary too, now."

Claire turned to look at him. She didn't know whether to be pleased he had wanted to take her for a drive, or disappointed and angry he had ruined everything, just to annoy his friend.

"Barton, you are a complete idiot," said his mother, "Sometimes you can be very clever and other times you can be very stupid. This is one of the stupid times and I don't know what we can do next. My first inclination was to send Miss Thompson home to minimise damage to our family reputation, her position as companion being temporary anyway. However, it's already too late to go today and she can't travel tomorrow because it will be Sunday.

When is the new governess starting?"

"Miss Fairfax starts on Monday morning. I had hoped there would be an overlap between Miss Fairfax and Miss Thompson to smooth the transition."

There was a long silence and Claire's heart sank even further. This was it then. She would be sent home on Monday, probably without a reference and without any chance to visit the agencies, not that there was much point in doing so now. She might as well start packing as soon as she went up to her room. Claire wondered if she should take all her new clothes with her, but obviously this was not the moment to ask. Perhaps it would be more tactful for Sally, her now very temporary lady's maid to ask Robbins, the dowager's lady's maid, what she should do. She had thought losing her position with Lady Sutton was a disaster, but it was as nothing compared to this.

"There is only one thing to do," said Lady Barton, "tomorrow we will all go to church at St George's and do so as conspicuously as possible. Barton, you will find Daintree this evening and insist he accompany us too. Perhaps if enough people see us all together, it might clarify the situation and shift the weight of opinion in our favour. You may both go away now and reflect upon your folly."

Claire rose, curtsied to her lady ship and followed Barton to the door which he opened for her.

"I apologise for my mistake, Miss Thompson," he said as he followed her out, "if her ladyship insists on you returning home on Monday, naturally you will use our carriage and you will be well paid for all your assistance."

"Thank you, my lord," she said, her voice muffled by tears which she was struggling to hold back. She hurried up to her room where she threw herself onto the bed and sobbed into her pillow.

Philippa Carey

Chapter 20 - Sunday

Claire had not seen the family again on Saturday, having asked for a tray in her room. Breakfast on Sunday was a sombre affair. Claire had gone to the breakfast room, realising she couldn't hide away in her room. She had to face the family and the servants too, for sooner or later they would all learn everything.

"Ives," said the countess to the butler who was serving her coffee, "you may have heard there is a ugly and entirely false rumour going the rounds concerning Miss Thompson, Lady Mary and Lord Daintree. In normal circumstances I would be annoyed if our staff were to gossip about the family with servants from other houses. However, in this case, if any of the staff were hear of this rumour during their afternoon off today, they may feel free to refute it as strongly as they wish."

"I understand, my lady, I shall address the staff during their breakfast."

"Furthermore, if any servants choose to attend the afternoon service at St George's rather than their usual church, it will be appreciated. I understand this may not be possible for those not of the Anglican faith or who may be required here in the house."

"I will pass on the suggestion my lady and will certainly attend St George's myself."

A sliver of hope appeared in Claire's heart as she looked up and listened to the instructions. It seemed

153

as though the dowager was making an effort to squash any rumour. Claire didn't know if the motivation was to avoid a stain on the Barton family reputation or on her reputation, or on both. She hadn't started packing her things last night, she had been too upset. She was in no mood to do it today either and besides, she didn't have much, so it could easily be done on Monday morning.

In the afternoon, they went to Hanover Square in the coach. As they arrived at the church, Claire could see Lord Daintree waiting for them by the pillars at the front. Further back, nearer to the church door, were Ives and a small group of the staff. One of the footmen hurried forward to let down the carriage steps. The earl descended first to help his mother down. He then lifted Lady Mary down before offering a hand to Claire.

"Daintree," said the dowager, "you will offer me your arm if you please. We will be sitting at the front."

Lord Daintree said nothing, having been briefed by Barton the evening before, but offered her his arm. They walked into the church followed by Claire, who was followed by Barton, holding Mary's hand. The servants then followed them in, led by Ives, but they took seats at the back.

As Claire walked up the aisle behind Daintree and the dowager she could hear whispers from the congregation who were already filling the pews. She couldn't hear what they said, but felt sure many of the whispers were about her. She resisted the temptation to glance around or to swallow nervously, carried her head high and looked resolutely forwards. Claire told herself she had nothing to be ashamed of and she carefully kept her face blank until they reached the front where she sat between the dowager and Lady Mary.

Chapter 21 - Monday

The next morning Claire was awash with anxiety. Lady Oswald was closeted with Lady Barton. Miss Fairfax, who felt like Claire's replacement, was due to arrive at any moment. Claire was with Lady Mary who seemed very irritable and strident this morning. Claire knew this was due to her own nervousness and difficulty in concentrating. She couldn't settle to anything and nor could Mary. On the one hand Claire resented the arrival of Miss Fairfax, but on the other hand, she felt some sympathy for the lady who was unwittingly going to walk into a anxious house full of bad tempered people.

Finally a footman appeared in the schoolroom to tell Claire that Lady Barton wanted to see her in her ladyship's sitting room. Claire went downstairs clutching her hands together to stop them trembling. When she arrived, she found Lady Oswald was still there as well as Lord Barton.

"Miss Thompson," said the dowager, "Lady Oswald believes the opinion of the ton may have swung in our favour. However, there will surely be some doubts remaining, so we need a further public demonstration to set the matter to rest."

"Barton," said the dowager, "You will accompany myself, Miss Thompson and Lady Mary for a drive in the barouche at the fashionable hour this afternoon."

So, thought the earl, it seems we are to provide some theatre to make our point.

"Does Miss Thompson have a suitably stylish carriage dress?" asked Lady Oswald.

"Eminently so. The modiste completed a number of gowns much earlier than I had expected. Now Miss Thompson will not embarrass us when we are seen together."

"Embarrass us?" asked Barton.

"Well, it is perhaps too harsh a word, but her gowns were sadly provincial. I don't suppose it would have mattered to the infamous Lady Sutton, tucked away in the depths of Buckinghamshire. However, here it town it does matter, because people will notice and it would have reflected badly upon you and me. Not only this, but Miss Thompson's Kentish gown will no doubt have added to the confusion over her relationship with Lord Daintree."

"Ah, so now we are fit to appear at the fashionable hour," said David, nodding sagely. It did not matter a great deal to him what people said about his appearance, he had nothing he felt he had to prove. He had no interest in being seen as a dandy, but instead, he thought some of Beau Brummel's ideas had merit and so he habitually dressed in rather plain black, grey and white. Extravagantly striped multicoloured waistcoats and heavily padded shoulders were definitely not his style. However, he knew his appearance did matter to his mother, so for this reason he cared how he dressed.

His mother's attention to the way they appeared, also explained why she was buying new gowns for Miss Thompson. A young lady who might have only been with them for another week or so. The cost to him of the dresses was neither here nor there, he could easily afford whatever his mother was likely to spend. Besides, if his mother was enjoying the shopping, then never mind the cost. The price of the behavioural improvement in Mary wrought by Miss Thompson was well worth it in any case. In addition, his mother might also feel a little guilty of the way they had imposed on Miss Thompson.

His mother had frowned at his sarcasm, but did not comment upon it.

Claire felt they were talking about her as if she wasn't there. However she clearly wasn't being sent home today and, as well, they were still working to restore her reputation, not merely their own. So she kept quiet and started to breathe again.

"I know most people have repaired to the country," said the dowager, "but we need to be seen. It will be also be useful for people to see you are no longer escorting Miss Hawksley."

Well, that was interesting, thought Claire. It might explain why Miss Hawksley had been looking daggers at Claire during the ball. Had Claire misunderstood, and she wasn't just being used at the ball to put Miss Hawksley's nose out of joint?

"You said we should take Mary," said Barton, "is this not a little irregular for the fashionable hour?"

"Yes," said his mother, "and it's a bit late for you to be thinking of it, after sending her with Daintree. However, now there is a reason for it. We shall stop and talk to anyone and everyone who is willing to speak to us. Then we will explain how the outing is by way of a treat for my granddaughter Lady Mary who is horse mad. I have no doubt her enthusiasm will show, particularly since we will not overly restrain her chatter and excitement. Clearly she cannot be anybody's natural daughter if she has a title. You, Barton, will take charge of Mary to emphasise, if need be, how you are her father. Then I shall introduce Miss Thompson as the daughter of Baron Hunton and how she is now my companion. This is all they need to know. It's none of their business as to why I suddenly have a companion. All in all, it should clarify who is whom and what our relationships are. If anybody still has doubts after that, they are simply idiots."

Claire relaxed at last. These people were obviously on her side and wanted to keep her, at least for the time being.

"Milady," said Claire, "how much should I say if I am spoken to?"

"As little as possible, just smile and nod if you don't have to answer a direct question. I shall deal with any nosey or impertinent questions."

Warned to say little, Claire was disappointed. It might have been a way to let it be known she was looking for a new post of companion. However, she resolved to listen carefully in case anything was let slip by any ladies looking for a companion. Who knew what they might say when talking to Lady Barton? Her having just acquired a companion after declaring she didn't want or need one might provoke some comment. One never knew one's luck, did one? After all, who would have guessed she would be here in Mayfair when she was supposed to be at Sutton Hall in the village of Wicken?

There was a light tap at the door and Ives opened it half-way.

"My lord, Miss Fairfax has arrived."

"Thank you Ives, we will be down directly." said Barton. He faced his mother and Lady Oswald. "If we are finished mother?"

She nodded. "Yes, the two of you may go."

"Good morning Lady Oswald and thank you for your assistance," he said.

Lady Oswald nodded to him and he turned to Claire.

"Miss Thompson, let us go and welcome Miss Fairfax."

Claire curtsied to the two ladies and followed him out of the door.

Late in the afternoon, Mary was left in the care of Maisie and Miss Fairfax to be dressed as smartly as possible. Claire went to her own room to change into her carriage dress. Not only Sally was there, but Robbins, Lady Barton's maid, had been sent as well, to ensure Claire looked her absolute best. Claire was then taken to see the dowager.

Lady Barton looked Claire up and down with a critical eye.

"Yes, very good, you'll do," she said, "we shall go down now."

Claire escorted her ladyship down to the front hall where Barton, Miss Fairfax and Lady Mary were waiting. Claire thought Lady Mary was looking very pretty and had no doubt Mary had also been inspected by the dowager. She thought Lord Barton looked exceedingly handsome and her heart skipped a beat. She knew she mustn't let her imagination run away with her, but if only they were a real family group, it would have been wonderful.

A footman assisted Lady Barton into the carriage, and Claire followed her. Claire went to sit with her back to the horses.

"No, Miss Thompson, you will sit with me. I don't want anyone to think you are the governess. You are the daughter of a peer and my companion. You will sit next to me."

Claire was a little surprised, as she had expected to sit facing backwards, either next to Lady Mary or Lord Barton. However, the countess's tone was not one which allowed of any argument.

Lady Mary climbed in and sat facing her grandmother. Barton sat next to her. He smiled at Claire who couldn't help smiling back before she dropped her eyes to the floor.

"Miss Thompson," said the dowager, "you will sit up straight and look as if you belong there if you please. Remember you are not the governess. And Barton, take the silly grin off your face, we may be on display, but this is not a harlequinade."

Claire looked at Barton with wide eyes. Her ladyship often had forthright views. However, today she was in a very imperious mood, not at all like her usual demeanour. Perhaps, just perhaps, she was feeling nervous and anxious too? Surely nobody would dare snub her or give them the cut? She noticed Barton was looking rather surprised at his mother's attitude too.

The earl was indeed feeling a little surprised, but not at his mother's commanding manner, he had seen it many times in the past. No, he was surprised at the reference to Harlequin. Whilst on the face of it, she was simply telling him this was not a comedy, was she also betraying her thoughts? Was he Harlequin to Miss Thompson's Columbine? His mother had arranged them in the carriage just as if they were a family group and Miss Thompson was his countess. As the barouche rolled away towards Hyde Park, he had a few minutes of quiet contemplation before they met other people, when he would have to listen to them and no doubt make sensible replies. Not to mention Lady Mary who would probably be bouncing up and down with excitement and she might need a little restraint from her father.

As he considered their arrangement in the carriage like a family, he realised that he had affection for Miss Thompson. He was also reminded of the way they would have looked like a family group at Astley's Amphitheatre. He had been distressed at the suggestion she would have been on her way home to Farleigh Green this afternoon. When he had said she would go in their travelling carriage, he had been thinking he would be going with her. Now the situation had cooled, he could see it would have been silly, made no sense at all and been completely improper too. However, it did show him he wanted her company. The idea she might have been leaving, had rattled him and he had been unable to concentrate on anything for the remainder of Saturday. He had ascribed it to the general air of tension and distress in the house. Maybe this hadn't been the full reason.

The horses were clip-clopping behind him and the wheels rumbled along the cobble-stoned street. He had been lost in thought, gazing into the distance as the street retreated behind the carriage. His attention was suddenly drawn to the lady in front of him, as the truth of the matter hit him in a burst of understanding. It wasn't merely a case of affection for his mother's companion. He was in love with her. He had been sub-consciously avoiding the question, skirting around the issue, pretending to himself it wasn't the case, because she was a servant. It was the sort of thing which couldn't be allowed in respectable households. Now he had to confront the knowledge of how he had been in love with her for some time.

Moreover, as his mother had just pointed out, she was not the governess and a companion wasn't really a servant either. Furthermore, she was the daughter of a baron and, as his mother had also commented moments ago, she did look as if she belonged there, just as if she was his countess. If he wasn't mistaken, Miss Thompson and Lady Mary had forged a bond like mother and daughter. He looked at Miss Thompson. She was looking directly at him and his brown eyes locked with her blue eyes. He couldn't help smiling at her. Everything was perfect. He loved her, she was beautiful and she would make the perfect countess. She smiled back at him, but somewhat tentatively. His euphoria wavered a little. It was only perfect if she cared for him too, and he wasn't sure on this point. She was kind and amiable, so everybody liked her. Perhaps she was no more than kind and amiable to him as well, and there was no particular affection there?

Claire couldn't help returning the earl's smile. He looked confident this drive in the park would quell the rumours. But would it really work? The dowager was nervous, and did her experience of the ton mean she knew better than this? Claire's nerve wobbled a little, but she sat up straight, told herself to concentrate, blinked several times and took a deep breath as they entered the gates of the park.

Moments later the carriage slowed and drew to a halt beside another carriage going in the opposite direction. In the next hour, Claire was introduced to a whole host of people whose names she was sure she would never remember. This time she didn't have a dance card to jog her memory. The earl occasionally exchanged greetings with those same people but mostly he was drawing Mary's attention to the other carriages, their horses and the horses of riders in the park. Some of the people they met frowned a little at Mary's presence and her obvious excitement, but others smiled indulgently at her. All were told she was the earl's daughter by his late wife and Claire did not see anyone having obvious doubts in the matter.

Finally they moved slowly out of the park and the carriage picked up speed as they headed back down Piccadilly towards home in Half Moon Street.

The dowager puffed out her cheeks and let out a breath in a rather un-ladylike manner.

"Thank goodness," she said, "I think it all went as well as we could have hoped."

She patted Claire's knee. "You did very well my dear, nobody will think now you are Daintree's.... Well, you know what I mean."

She cocked an eye in Mary's direction, but Mary wasn't listening anyway. She was still chattering to her father about all the horseflesh she had seen and how she needed a pony in London so she could ride in Hyde Park as well. The earl was nodding sceptical agreement to everything she said. At length he interrupted her monologue.

"Mary, it won't be long before we go back to Hemingford Park. Moonbeam must be wondering where you are and how you might have forgotten how to ride her."

"No," said Mary, horrified, "I won't have forgotten how to ride and Moonbeam won't have forgotten me either."

"Good, and then when you start riding lessons again, we shall have to find a horse for Miss Thompson, so she can take lessons with you."

"Yes, papa, that will be very nice. I shall like it very much," she said, smiling at Claire, "when can we go home?"

"Oh, I don't know, not long I expect."

Claire opened her mouth to remind him it would be Miss Fairfax riding with Mary, not her. Then she closed it again. It might be a matter of regret she would not be going back to Hemingford Park, but still, it was just a slip of the tongue. There was no need to correct him. Besides, this was not the time to

166

talk about it with Mary. Let her get used to Miss Fairfax first.

"Barton," said the dowager as they drew up outside the house. "I am in the mood to go to the theatre this evening. Find out if you please what is on. You may escort myself and Miss Thompson."

Everybody understood 'may' meant 'will', so he merely nodded as the steps were being let down. As they entered the house, Maisie and Miss Fairfax were waiting for Mary. Barton had a word with Ives. Claire and her ladyship made their way upstairs to their rooms.

After she had changed and before going down to dinner, Claire went up to the nursery. Mary was being prepared for bed by Maisie and Miss Fairfax. Maisie was brushing Mary's hair while Miss Fairfax sat beside her.

"Miss Thompson, we've had a splendid time haven't we?" said Mary with a broad grin, "I'm telling Miss Fairfax all about it."

Mary had turned her head to the door and so Maisie paused in her brushing.

"Lady Mary says she saw hundreds of horses," added Miss Fairfax, suppressing a grin.

"Did I tell you about the really, really, big one which was all black?" said Mary, turning back.

Maisie resumed the brushing and Claire retreated towards the stairs. She was relieved because Mary seemed to have accepted Miss Fairfax, but disappointed because now it was one less reason for her to be retained in the household.

Whilst they had pre-dinner drinks, Barton said a box had been secured for them at the Drury Lane Theatre to watch Edmund Kean perform as Shylock in The Merchant of Venice.

"Very good, this will do nicely," said the dowager, "Kean is always worth watching. Have you seen him before Miss Thompson?"

"No indeed not, although I have heard of him. Our nearest theatre was in Maidstone and it is rather small. We only had infrequent visits from travelling companies, which I very much doubt were up to London standards."

"You may find Kean a revelation in that case. In don't know about Maidstone, but tonight there will be many people looking to see who is in our box. This is perfectly normal and you may be entirely relaxed about it. It is why we make sure we look our best when we attend. I'm quite sure we scotched that silly rumour this afternoon, but there may be some comment when we are observed. However it will only confirm we have nothing to hide."

"If the theatre in Maidstone was small, you may be surprised at the size of Drury Lane," said Barton, "I believe there is space for nearly three thousand spectators."

"Three thousand?" said Claire, "goodness me, it must be ten times the size of Maidstone!"

"Not as large as the one which burnt down," said the dowager, "but by all accounts, the new one has been fireproofed, so we may rest easy on that score."

As they entered the box at Drury Lane, Claire looked around in amazement. It was huge. At least they had a good position, close to the stage, so she would be able to see and hear everything. She saw boxes further back were very large, but their's had only three seats at the front and a couple at the back for their maids. The dowager sat nearest the stage and Claire in the middle. This suited Barton admirably as he could watch the stage, or when it was less interesting, watch Miss Thompson instead. He contemplated what he should do next, if he was to gain her hand in marriage. A drive in the park would seem to be a simple start.

In the event, he had no chance to ask her before they had got home and gone up to bed. No matter, he could ask in the morning.

Philippa Carey

Chapter 22 - Tuesday

But on Tuesday morning he was besieged by first Ives, then Trevor, both needing his full attention. Finally it was nearing three o'clock and if he was to ask her, it had to be now.

"Ives," he said, leaving his study and entering the hall, "where might I find Miss Thompson?"

"I believe she is upstairs in the drawing room with her ladyship," he said, "they are..." His voice trailed off as the earl was already bounding up the stairs. "... entertaining some lady visitors," finished Ives rather weakly.

Barton entered the drawing room expecting to find only his mother and her companion. He came to a sudden halt as he saw there were another six, seven, no, eight other ladies in the room.

"Ah, Barton, so good of you to join us," said his mother, in what he suspected was a gleeful voice.

He glanced at Miss Thompson who had paused in the act of pouring another cup of tea. If he was not mistaken, there was a twinkle in her eye and she was also amused by his sudden discomfiture. So much for his plan to take her driving, because he could see she had to remain and assist his mother. He also had to remain, at least for a short while, and make polite noises to the visitors. To make matters worse, some of them had brought daughters with them. Presumably the word had gone around that he was no longer courting Miss Hawksley. He saw he was a prime example of fools rushing in where angels fear

171

to tread.

"Would you care for tea my lord?" asked Miss Thompson with a raised eyebrow and a wickedly innocent look on her face."

"Er, no, thank you Miss Thompson, I cannot stay long, as there are, er, urgent matters I must attend to."

The devil. And if he didn't get out of here soon, there might be more ladies arriving and more daughters too. He could be stuck here the whole afternoon. This was presumably a side-effect of their parade in the park where they had stopped to talk to absolutely everybody, and now everybody felt they could call on them. Especially if they had marriageable daughters.

He moved around the room as quickly as decently possible, making sure he didn't get trapped in long conversations, and then made his escape. Just as he was about to descend back to his study, he heard the front door open and yet more visitors arrive. He beat a hasty retreat to the his late wife's sitting room. Nobody would look for him there, he could see the street, and with the door slightly ajar, he could hear visitors entering and leaving the drawing room. As soon as the coast was clear, he hurried downstairs, collected his hat, gloves and cane, and strode rapidly down the street. The refuge of his club was only a ten minute walk away.

That evening he was first down before dinner and Claire followed shortly afterwards.

"Ah, Miss Thompson, I had hoped to speak with you earlier, but it was not the time nor the place."

Claire raised an eyebrow in enquiry.

"The visitors," he offered in explanation.

"Ah yes. I did notice you made an escape as soon as you could."

He grinned ruefully.

"Yes, indeed. I had been intending to ask if I might take you for a drive in the park tomorrow?"

Claire stilled. She didn't know what to answer. On the one hand, yes, she would like nothing better than to be driven in the park by his lordship. On the other hand, after all the trouble they had gone to, what would people say?

"I don't know, my lord," she stammered, "would it not be improper?"

Just then the dowager joined them and they both faced her as she took a sherry from the butler.

"Mother," said Barton, "I have asked Miss Thompson to drive with me tomorrow, but she had doubts about the propriety of it. What is your opinion?"

The dowager sipped her sherry thoughtfully before answering.

"It will be an open carriage and we have established beyond any doubt exactly who and what Miss Thompson is, so I think it is permissible. Naturally Mary will not go with you."

"But my lady," said Claire, "will people not start making wild assumptions?"

"They may. However, if there are no obvious consequences, I'm sure they will soon forget about it."

Claire still had doubts. She wanted to go for the drive, but why did he? Was it to make up for the disastrous outing with Lord Daintree? He couldn't be courting her? No, this was preposterous. Never mind, If nothing else, she would have more to tell her sister in the next letter.

"Very well, my lord, thank you, I accept."

"We received several invitations today," continued the dowager, "and I have accepted the one for the Motson's ball tomorrow evening on behalf of us all. Miss Thompson, you will have to wear the same ball gown again, but it suited you very well, so do not worry about it."

Yet another ball? Thought Claire. She hadn't expected to attend the first ball, never mind another one only a few days later. And wearing the same gown again was not something she would worry about. At home she only had one good ball gown anyway. Her next letter home was going to be a long one.

Chapter 23 - Wednesday

The next afternoon, Claire and Barton set off for Hyde Park in his curricle. Claire was still assailed by doubts about the wisdom of this expedition. It wasn't too late for them to turn around or go somewhere else.

"My lord," she said, "would it be better for us to go to Green Park instead of Hyde Park?"

"Green Park? Why would we go to Green Park?"

"Because there will be many fewer people and so much less talk."

"Less talk?"

"Yes, you know. As to why you are driving me, of all people, in the park."

"Why I am driving you, Miss Thompson, is because I want to. It is an opportunity for us to talk without other people listening. Everywhere else there are people, servants, guests or whoever, all ready to eavesdrop. I also have no intention of stopping every ten yards to chatter to all and sundry."

So saying, he pulled his carriage out of the slow moving queue of carriages and took an entirely different line. Claire looked around as his horses trotted across the grass. Surely this would make them more obvious?

"But my lord, this will cause even greater speculation."

"Let them speculate. It is perfectly normal for a gentleman to be taking an attractive young lady for a drive in the park. They know who you are. They know who I am. And, frankly, I don't care what they say."

Claire looked sideways at him with her mouth slightly open. She didn't know what to make of this.

"Not only this," he said, drawing the horses to a stop, "but I would really like it if you would stop calling me 'my lord'. Please call me Barton as I asked you once before, and as do my friends and my family. I would like it even better if you would call me David."

She stared at him. He sounded techy, but he was inviting a familiarity she wasn't expecting and she was dumbfounded. On top of this, he didn't care if people were talking about the two of them and guessing what their relationship might really be? Was he then seriously intending to court her? No, surely not. She had wondered about it yesterday, but not really believed it could be the case. It was definitely not an unwelcome idea, but it was certainly a surprise.

They looked at each other in silence for quite some time, then a smiling Barton started his horses moving again.

"So Miss Thompson, do you think Mary and Miss Fairfax will deal well together?" he said as the horses walked slowly across the park.

"I hope so my... Barton, I told Miss Fairfax what had happened before and how a more positive and sympathetic and... and caring approach seemed to work much better. So far they seem to be getting along very well, so I am optimistic."

"If I am not mistaken, you care a great deal for

Mary yourself."

"Yes, I do. She has a quick temper and a rebellious nature sometimes, but after all, she is only a young child. The rest of the time she is a very lovable girl. I shall miss her when I am gone."

"I don't think you need worry about leaving, if you don't wish to."

Claire looked at him from the corner of her eye and wondered exactly what he meant. It seemed his intentions were serious, but why? She said she cared for Mary, but he hadn't taken the opportunity to say he cared for Claire herself. He needed to get an heir, as Mary couldn't inherit, which meant he needed to marry. He obviously hadn't wanted to marry Miss Hawksley so he had to find someone else. Did he see Claire as conveniently here and available? Someone who would make a suitable wife, a tolerable companion? As much as Claire understood that she loved him, it had to be mutual. Marrying him and hoping he would grow to love her might be a very foolish mistake. No, she had to be sure his feelings were more than mere friendship before allowing matters to go further.

"I don't suppose Lady Barton will need me any more after you all return to Hemingford Park. Now you have found a suitable governess, there is little to stop you returning, is there?"

"There is no hurry for us to return to Hemingford Park, and I am sure my mother will like to retain your company for a long time yet. I would say she has become fond of you and I would hope it is mutual."

"Yes, it is. I do not know how I would have found

Lady Sutton, but I'm happy to have become companion to Lady Barton, whether it is to be for a short time or longer. She is a very amiable lady."

Claire thought he had had ample opportunity to express some sort of affection for her, but they seemed to have wandered off the point. Perhaps she was right and it was only a question of convenience for him.

"As much as I am enjoying this drive I am conscious ladies take longer to prepare themselves for a ball than gentlemen. Then, since we are to dine first, I suppose I must take us home and not tarry here in the park. I am hoping you will reserve the first two waltzes for me this evening."

Claire was more than happy to waltz with him, but even more she wanted the supper dance with him.

"Certainly I shall, Barton. Are you sure you want two waltzes, even if the supper dance is not a waltz?"

"Ah. You make a good point. It is a dilemma. I suppose you will be obliged to escort my mother into supper in any case, so if another gentleman takes you both into supper, then my jealousy will be muted."

"Jealousy?"

"Certainly. And as I said to Mary, I would hope for more than two dances one day."

Claire's eyes widened. Goodness. What was he saying? Now Claire was getting confused. She looked to her side to find him looking intently back at her. An angry shout from the street drew his attention back to his horses and the traffic.

This time, as they waited in the receiving line for a ball, Claire didn't feel quite so overawed. Now she understood the routine at a grand ball and she suspected most of the people were mostly the same people as last time. However she wasn't very good at remembering people's names. She would have to avoid saying a gentleman's name until he had written it on her card. However, this wouldn't work for the ladies. She leant slightly towards Lady Barton and whispered.

"My lady, when we meet other ladies, do you suppose you could whisper their names to me before we greet them?"

The dowager, glanced at Claire with a conspiratorial smile and nodded.

Once they had entered the ballroom and Claire had collected her dance card, Barton wasted no time in writing his name against the first waltz and the supper dance. They shared a small smile because the supper dance was another waltz.

Barton stood beside his mother's chair and watched as Claire was borne away into the set for a country dance.

"Barton," said his mother quietly, "don't stand here looking like an abandoned puppy unless you want to start unnecessary gossip. You met a number of girls yesterday afternoon. You would do well to ask one or two of them to dance."

He was roused from his thoughts of Miss Thompson to awareness of a number of ladies around the room lacking partners. He caught the eye of one whom he recognised from his mother's afternoon tea and went over to her.

"Miss Grey," he said to her, "may I have the honour of this dance?"

As they joined the set, he couldn't help looking up the line of ladies to where Miss Thompson was facing her partner and waiting for the set to be filled. She glanced for a moment in his direction, gave a little smile and turned back to face her partner.

Barton faced his own partner to see that she was looking at him with an amused expression on her face and a raised eyebrow. He gave a little sheepish shrug of his shoulders and she grinned back before adopting a more neutral expression. He must be more circumspect, he thought, and not wear his heart on his sleeve. At least Miss Grey didn't seem to be offended. She was also a rather attractive young lady. It appeared she not only had confidence, but a sense of humour too. If he hadn't felt like a fox surrounded by hounds in his mother's drawing room, he might have paid more attention. As it was, his affections were fully engaged elsewhere. He resisted the temptation to look back up the set to Miss Thompson. However, he could imagine how Miss Grey and Daintree might well suit each other. Were they acquainted? If not, there might be a good turn he could do for both of them at the end of this dance. Furthermore, if Daintree took an interest in Miss Grey it might steer him away from Miss Thompson. In any case, Daintree seemed to be keeping his distance after the earlier incident. Barton had only met him at their club and he hadn't called at the house again.

The band struck a chord and he bowed to his

partner.

He did his duty with a variety of wallflowers whilst waiting impatiently for the first waltz. Finally he was bowing over Miss Thompson's hand and leading her onto the dance floor. Yet again during a waltz, they said nothing, but as he gazed down into her blue eyes, he was quite sure she was his destiny. It was fortunate the floor was not crowded with other dancers, as they would certainly have collided with another couple, neither of them having eyes for anyone else. Turning at the corner must have happened without conscious thought too. The music ended, she curtsied and he bowed before kissing her fingers. Her eyes widened, but she said nothing and he was past caring who else might have noticed. He was clear in his mind. He needed to speak with her father as soon as possible.

The supper waltz arrived after only another two country dances. Afterwards, as he led her towards the dining room, he was content to think he would be doing so many times in the future.

"Oh, wait," said Claire, pulling him to a halt, "should we not be taking her ladyship with us?"

Barton looked back into the ballroom. He was so wrapped up in Miss Thompson, he had completely forgotten about his mother. No doubt she would give them both a scold when they found her. Through the moving throng, he caught a glimpse of his mother standing next to Lady Oswald and they were both looking in his direction. Far from looking annoyed, they both had smiles on their faces. His mother waved them onward towards the dining room.

"It appears, Miss Thompson, like last time, my mother and Lady Oswald have no need of us. Come, let us go and find a small table."

Unfortunately for Barton's plans, there were no small tables left. However, a larger table occupied by Daintree and Miss Grey still had two chairs free. He wondered if his earlier supposition about them might have been correct.

"May we join you?" he asked.

"Please do," replied Daintree, rising to his feet, "Miss Thompson, have you met Miss Grey?"

"Yes, indeed we have, I'm pleased to see you again," said Claire, shaking hands with her.

"Daintree, shall we get some plates for the ladies?" asked Barton.

"Miss Grey, I'm pleased to see you here. I've only been in London a matter of days and know hardly anybody."

"Me too, we came to London a month ago and we've had few invitations, so I haven't met many people either. I was hoping we might become friends."

"I should like that, but I don't know how long I shall be here."

Miss Grey raised an eyebrow in question.

"Lady Barton doesn't really need a companion. She only employed me in order to return a favour. As soon as they go back to Buckinghamshire she won't need me any more. I shall have to find employment with another lady. Who knows who she might be? Or where she might live? Even if she lives in London, I don't suppose I will be attending many balls like this. Lady Barton has been very kind to me and I appreciate it."

"I see. It will be disappointing if you move away. If you remain in London I hope I could still visit you."

"I should like that. You must give me your direction so we can stay in touch, even if I have to go home to Kent. Had you met Lord Daintree before?" said Claire.

"No. I understand he is a good friend of Lord Barton, who introduced us."

"He is and he is a very charming gentleman too."

"Yes. I must confess I am rather attracted to him and wonder why we had never met before. I noticed you and Lord Barton seem rather taken with each other too."

"You did?" said Claire, feeling her face flushing.

"Why yes, I expect everyone noticed. My mother won't allow me to waltz yet, so I was watching the dancers. You two were in a world of your own."

"Oh," said Claire. She hadn't realised it would be quite so obvious.

"Now I see it was a waste of time my mother pushing me in front of Lord Barton yesterday afternoon."

"It was?"

"Certainly, if there is to be an announcement soon." Miss Grey suddenly put her hand to her mouth and looked horrified. "Oh dear, I've let my mouth run away with me and I've been impertinent, haven't I? I'm so sorry, my besetting sin is saying things without thinking first. Please forgive me!"

"Of course, but don't expect any announcement. He's not going to offer for me when I have nothing to bring to a marriage. If I had any sort of dowry or connections I wouldn't be a lady's companion, would I?"

"No, I suppose not."

"As it is, I'm just enjoying the balls, the theatre and so on, whilst I have the chance."

Just then the gentlemen arrived back with a plate of food in each hand.

Chapter 24 - Thursday

Claire and the dowager had moved to the morning room after breakfast.

"Miss Thompson, how are Miss Fairfax and Lady Mary progressing?"

"They seem to getting along very well. Lady Mary's previous governess took a harsh approach, from what I can gather, and Lady Mary rebelled rather than buckle under. Consequently I advised Miss Fairfax to take a gentler approach, as it had seemed to work for me. As far as I can see they are dealing with each other famously."

"Very good, I am very pleased. I imagine your experience with younger siblings helped you to take the right approach at the beginning."

"Probably so. My younger brothers were difficult from time to time as well."

"Now, Miss Thompson, Barton has gone out of own," said Lady Barton, "and this evening we shall ttend the opera."

"Will his lordship be back in time for it?"

"No, he won't be back until tomorrow. In any case, he doesn't care for it. Now you are here I can go without him and he will no doubt be glad to miss it. Do you enjoy the opera?"

"I don't know milady, I've never been."

"Never been? Goodness me, I suppose then they do not have opera in Maidstone?"

"Not as far as I am aware. I imagine the town is too small to warrant it."

"In this case you may find it educational. The opera is Artaxerxes which is in English rather than Italian, this being a small mercy, especially since the plot is very complicated. I can tell you what it is about, but even so, you may need to concentrate if the pit is particularly raucous."

"The people in the pit in the Maidstone theatre were sometimes noisy, but it never stopped us hearing the play."

"I'm afraid the audiences here are more interested in being seen rather than seeing the play or the opera. Consequently they make a lot of noise to be heard over everybody else making noise. Since the opera house is so large, the clamour is enormous. It can be like Bedlam sometimes. Fortunately we will again have a box near the stage, so this should help."

"Have you seen this opera before milady?"

"Yes, several times, although I can't say it's my favourite. However there is not much else on at the moment and so I thought we may as well see this one."

Ah, thought Claire, this sounds like she is not going to wait for some other opera, one which is more to her taste. Is this a hint they will soon be going back to the country? As well as this, her ladyship was asking if Miss Fairfax was satisfactory. Since she is, presumably there is nothing now to stop them returning. Possibly it only requires for Barton to finish his business and return tomorrow before they pick a return date. Perhaps she should start doing something now about finding a new post.

Claire wondered if her new friend Miss Grey might have any suggestions. She decided to send her a note without delay.

As Claire considered how she might be leaving soon, she thought of Lady Mary. Now Miss Fairfax was here, she wasn't spending so much time with Mary.

"If you will excuse me, my lady, there are a couple of letters I should write this morning."

"Of course, you run along while I read the newspaper."

Instead of going straight to her room, Claire went up to the nursery, where she found Miss Fairfax and Lady Mary sitting at a table. Mary was drawing a picture.

"Good morning Mary, good morning Miss Fairfax."

"Miss Thompson, look I'm drawing a picture," said Mary, holding the picture up so Claire could see. The picture was being held upside-down, but Claire could see it was a creature with four spindly legs.

"Oh it's very nice," said Claire, "it looks just like Moonbeam."

Miss Fairfax smiled and gave a little nod of confirmation.

"Yes," said Mary, "and as soon as we get home I will take it to the stables to show Fingle and Moonbeam." She put the paper back down on the table and bent over it industriously.

Claire nodded at Miss Fairfax, smiled weakly and

left the nursery. More confirmation, she thought as she went down a floor to her own room. Even Mary knew they were leaving soon. As well as a note for Miss Grey, she should probably send a note to the agency which had sent her to Lady Sutton. Hopefully, after the previous debacle, they would make more strenuous efforts to find her a suitable position. Claire had intended to write to her sister and father too, but since his lordship was away she wouldn't get a frank for the letter. In this case, she thought, it might as well wait until tomorrow when she could tell her sister about the opera too. However, she could still write the two notes, because a footman could deliver them.

As they entered their box at the opera, Claire could hear what the dowager meant about noise. She peered over the edge of the box to see the people in the pit below.

"Goodness me, what a hubbub," she exclaimed to Lady Barton, "everybody is milling about down there instead of sitting on the benches. And who are those men strutting up and down?"

The dowager looked to where Claire was pointing.

"Fops, my dear, fops. They call the aisle 'fops alley'. Pay no attention, they are not people with whom we associate."

Claire looked around at the other boxes. They were all well filled and in more than one, somebody was holding a pair of opera glasses to their eyes. If she was not mistaken, they were looking in her direction. She sat back rather abruptly and focussed on the stage, not that there was anything to see there for the moment.

"Pay no attention, Miss Thompson," said the dowager, "they are just inquisitive and wanting to see who is here. We were last week's news, so this week we are of little interest. Next week they will have forgotten all about us."

Especially, thought Claire, since we won't be here. She applied herself to the opera and everything which was going on, so she could describe it all in tomorrow's letter to her sister.

Philippa Carey

Chapter 25 - Friday

The earl was back and since he could frank her letter, Claire was writing a long one to her family, not having to worry about the cost. There was a knock at her door and she turned to see a footman there.

"If you please miss, Lord Barton asks if you would attend him in his study when convenient."

Claire nodded and put her pen down. She blotted the page. The letter wasn't finished, but she would undoubtedly have more to add after seeing his lordship. She felt sure this was the moment he was going to tell her when the family were going back to Hemingford Park. She would then be free to take up a new post and, with a bit of luck, she might hear from Miss Grey or the agency later today. She hoped she could find a new position promptly. If not, she would be going home to Farleigh Green in the meantime. She stood, smoothed down her dress, took a deep breath and headed downstairs.

"My lord, you wanted to see me?"

"Ah yes," said Barton standing up, "please close the door behind you."

Claire hesitated.

"I have something to say to you of a personal nature and don't wish everyone to hear it."

Clearly she was to get her marching orders, which was why he appeared a little nervous. Telling somebody they were no longer needed couldn't be a pleasant thing to do. She clicked the door closed and turned back to find he had come closer across the room.

"Miss Thompson, over the last week or two I have felt we got along together very well and I wonder if you would do me the honour of becoming my wife."

Claire was rooted to the spot and her mouth dropped open in a most unbecoming way. She stared at him with wide eyes. What did he say? Did he just ask her to marry him? Surely she misheard him?

"I beg your pardon my lord?" she said, frowning in confusion.

"Will you marry me, Miss Thompson?" he said with a slight smile.

A blunt marriage proposal was the last thing Claire had been expecting to hear and she had to gather her thoughts for a moment.

"But why? Why do you want to marry me?" she asked.

He was taken aback and the smile slipped from his face.

"Well, as I said, I thought we dealt well together and both Mary and my mother both like you. Then as well, I thought you liked them, and me too..., and..., and besides, your background is very suitable."

These were not the reasons Claire would have liked to hear as the reason for an offer of marriage. She loved him but if the sentiment wasn't returned, it was a bad basis for marriage. She had thought he might love her, but he hadn't said so and she could be mistaken in him. If he fell in love with another woman at a later date, it would make life very unhappy for his wife. She knew such marriages existed, but she didn't want to enter one like them herself. No, the love had to be mutual. She knew he had to marry someone and it appeared he thought she was suitable. Conveniently, she was also already here and so he wouldn't have to look any further. But it wasn't enough. She was so dazed she said aloud what she was thinking.

"I suppose, it is also convenient that I am already here."

"Well, yes, I suppose it is convenient," he said slowly and hesitantly.

So, as she thought, she was merely suitable and conveniently available. This was no good.

"Thank you for your offer, my lord, but I cannot accept. If you will excuse me, I must now speak with her ladyship."

Claire curtsied briefly, and then left him standing there as she hurried out of the study.

She ran up to her room, closed her door and threw herself onto the bed. Tears rolled down her cheeks. She had hoped he might love her, but he obviously didn't. She had to leave tomorrow. She couldn't stay any longer, it would be too embarrassing and the family were leaving soon in any case. She had no chance or time to find an alternative, so she had to go home. There simply wasn't time to get a reply from the agency or Miss Grey either, so she would have to write to them again from Farleigh Green. Oh, why did he have to spoil it all? She would have left in a few days with regrets, but she would have had happy memories to help her get over them. Now she couldn't even write to Lady Mary when she was employed elsewhere. It would be quite unacceptable, especially when he married someone else. After all, it wouldn't be hard for him to find some other lady willing to marry him. Like Miss Hawksley for example. But first she had to tender her resignation to Lady Barton. She slid off the bed to get the jug of water on the washstand. She had to rinse her undoubtedly red eyes in cold water and regain her composure before going in search of her ladyship.

In the meantime, Lady Barton looked up eagerly as her son entered her sitting room. She heaved a sigh upon seeing his downcast face.

"I can see you bungled it and she refused you."

He nodded wryly.

"What precisely did you say to her?"

Barton looked embarrassed and shrugged. La[dy] Barton was reminded of when he was a small bo[y] and hadn't wanted to admit a mistake.

"Come, come," she said, "this is no time to be[...] unless you want to lose her. You don't do you?"

He opened and closed his mouth a couple of times before shaking his head.

"Well then? What did you say?"

"I said how we all liked her and how she was eminently suitable and she and I got along well together... and I asked her to marry me."

"And?"

"And she asked if it was convenient that she was here."

The dowager closed her eyes. She could see it all.
He could be much too reserved for his own good.
"So I suppose you said 'yes, it was convenient'.
Barton, you are such a prize idiot and not for the
first time. Did you tell her you loved her?"
He looked very uncomfortable as he thought over
what he had actually said.
"As I said only the other day Barton, you can be
very clever. Other times you can be completely
stupid. Your father was the same. This, I regret, is
another one of those times when you are being an
imbecile. You didn't tell her the single most
important thing. I'm not surprised she refused you
when you said she was convenient and not about
how you love her. You do love her you know, even I
can see the truth of it. You stay here and I shall go to
find Miss Thompson. While I am gone, you should
think very carefully about how you feel. You may get
a second chance, but likely not a third one."

The dowager hurried out of the room only to find
Claire coming the other way down the hall.

"Ah, Miss Thompson, the very person! Come into
my sitting room please."

"Your ladyship, I..."

"Yes, yes," interrupted the dowager, "tell me
everything in a moment. In the meantime Barton
forgot to tell you something."

She pushed Claire unceremoniously into the
room and closed the door behind her. She hoped her
son had the wit to retrieve the situation before it was
too late.

Claire stumbled into the room and, looking

behind her, saw the dowager had shut her in. Shut her in with Lord Barton.

"Miss Thompson, I have been a complete and unmitigated fool by not telling you the real reason I want to marry you."

"No my lord, please say no more, I cannot marry you," said Claire putting her hands up as if to hold him off.

"But Miss Thompson, I love you most ardently, and I was so nervous when I spoke to you before, I neglected to tell you so. My love for you is the principle reason for my asking you and if you were to leave me, I would be entirely bereft."

Claire hesitated. Did he really love her or was he just saying it at his mother's prompting? She was tempted, but could she be sure?

"But Barton, how can you want to marry me when I bring nothing to the marriage? I have nothing, no dowry, not even any useful connections."

"You have brought light and warmth into our lives. Most of all, you bring yourself and this is all I really care about. I love you and I want you beside me forever. I am desperately hoping you might love me too and will say you will marry me. Will you?"

She had wondered before if he might be in love with her. Now he looked sincere, he sounded sincere and she was convinced he was sincere.

"Yes, I do love you. I have done for a while. And yes, I will marry you, but only if you start calling me Claire instead of Miss Thompson."

He took her hands and leant in to kiss her.

"Wait!" she said, leaning backwards, "you must

ask my father first."

"Claire, I already did, so please let me kiss you."

"You did? When?"

"Yesterday," he said, finally capturing her lips for a tender kiss.

After a minute or two, there was a loud click and they moved apart, although only slightly.

"What was that?" she asked.

"Nothing," said Barton, looking over her shoulder, "merely the door which hadn't been properly closed."

"I suppose we should tell your mother."

"Oh, I think she has probably guessed. We should go and tell Mary as well."

They went up to the nursery, hand-in-hand. When they opened the door, Mary saw them and came running over.

"Papa! Miss Thompson!"

They crouched down in front of her.

"Mary," said Barton, "I have asked Miss Thompson to marry me and she has agreed. She is going to be your new mama. Will you like this?"

Mary looked at her father with wide eyes and an open mouth as she thought about it. Then she turned to Claire, and studied her for a short moment. Then she flung her arms about Claire's neck and said "my mama!"

Claire cuddled Mary close, then with glistening eyes and a crooked smile, she looked over Mary's head to Barton.

The End

Philippa Carey

Historical Notes

In the Regency, Stony Stratford was a very busy little town. Over thirty stage and mail coaches stopped there every day on their way between London and Chester, Birmingham, Liverpool and Manchester. Then, as well as the north-south traffic, there was more traffic east-west between Cambridge, Norwich, Oxford, Bath and Bristol. When you add in the private coaches, riders on horseback and goods vehicles, it is easy to see it would have been a hive of activity with horses being changed and travellers getting refreshments or stopping overnight. There were over a dozen coaching inns in a very short High Street, so on average it was about one inn every fifty yards. Then there were large requirements for supplies such as food and drink for travellers and more for the horses and vehicles, which accounts for the more than fifty establishments serving the passing trade.

In this hubbub of activity, it is easy to see how the identity of a traveller could be mistaken.

Two of the coaching inns were the Cock Inn and the Bull Inn, no more than a few yards apart. It is said that gossip would arrive on the coaches and then go back and forth between the two inns, gradually getting more and more embellished. Hence the expression 'A Cock and Bull Story'.

There is also the nursery rhyme "Ride a Cock Horse to Banbury Cross". It has been suggested this may refer to a horse rented from the Cock Inn, since it is about a day's horse ride to Banbury Cross.

About the Author

Philippa Carey graduated from Cambridge University as a Software Engineer, later becoming an entrepreneur, then a driver of heavy goods vehicles. Philippa is now semi-retired, writing and living near Cambridge in the United Kingdom.

Philippa is a member of the Romantic Novelist's Association and RNA author profiles can be found here:
www.romanticnovelistsassociation.org/rna_author

Look for more of Philippa's novels and novellas, which are set in a mixture of The Regency, the Victorian era, World War One and the present day.

To see what is currently available, go to
www.pcarey.uk

If you would leave a review of this novel wherever you bought it, Philippa will be eternally grateful.